GROWING BY FOUR FEET

A STORY ABOUT FAMILY

CARMEN KLASSEN

ETA Publishing Ltd

Growing by Four Feet

Success on Her Terms Book 7

By Carmen Klassen

CONTENTS

CHAPTER 1

Carrie took a deep breath and focused on her job as she clicked on the screen to call her last client of the day. A few seconds later, Alicia's face popped up—pale, dark circles under her eyes, and her hair was pulled to the side in a low ponytail instead of her usual carefully blown out style.

"Hi Carrie."

"Hi Alicia. How is today?"

"Ugh. Not good. People suck." She took a drink from an awful looking concoction in a glass.

"That drink looks like it might be part of your problem!"

Alicia made a face. "It's another of Brian's great ideas. He's got me on some fertility diet."

"I'm guessing that's not part of the 'people suck' portion of your life, though."

"Not at all. I can live with eating and drinking anything if it will get me pregnant. But I'm not sure how much longer I can live with people's ignorant comments. We were at Brian's friend's place for dinner last night. They have three kids. I think the wife could be a good friend, but the guy? Total jerk. All night he kept making jokes about whether Brian knew what he was doing in the bedroom, and if he needed some pointers. It was so crass."

"And it's still bothering you today?"

"Totally. Why can't people just focus on us as people? I swear, the next person who tells us we just need to practice more is going to get an earful of nasty."

Carrie's heart went out to Alicia. It was something she was already starting to deal with in her own life, as every month since getting remarried she had a reminder that she wasn't pregnant. She rubbed her hands on her legs and tried to keep her attention on Alicia.

"I know we've talked a lot about your choices, and what you can and can't control, but it sounds like this is a good time to talk about other people. It's actually an extension of this concept that we can only control ourselves. Are you with me?"

Alicia nodded, and took another drink from her cup with a grimace as she swallowed.

"OK, since we can't control others, their behaviors—and in situations like last night, their words especially—are never personal. As women we've been programmed to take what other people say personally, but it doesn't have to be like that. Because when other people say things, they are really just giving us information about themselves."

"So this guy's giving me information that he's a total jerk?"

Carrie smiled. "Kind of. But it's more about what we choose to internalize and what we choose to compartmentalize as something that isn't about us. He gave you information about how he handles other people's personal issues and whether he'd be someone you want to have a connection with—or not, as the case may be."

"I kind of get what you're saying, but I'm so emotional that I *do* take all those comments to heart."

"And what do you tell yourself when you've taken in all those comments?"

"I start to think that I'm a failure." Her chin quivered. "That I'm doing something wrong, or that I *am* something wrong and that's why I'm not pregnant."

"OK, and are those thoughts facts?"

Alicia shook her head.

"Are they true?" Carrie asked gently.

There was a pause. "No, they're not true."

"So this is where everything ties in together. When you take everything others say to heart, you give them control over you. You allow your thoughts to swirl around the things they've said, and you start to think in ways that deepen the hurt.

"But when you decide that other people's words are just information, you're far less likely to take them to heart. Add that to the practice of being conscious about what you think, and stopping yourself when your thoughts aren't true and helpful, and you become empowered and resilient."

Now it was Alicia's turn to smile. "That's one of my favorite words —resilient."

Carrie did an internal fist pump. In her notes from their first conversation she had noticed how Alicia responded to that word. She was glad her observation was accurate.

"I totally agree. It's a great word to hang on to, especially with what you and Brian are going through right now. Taking control of your thoughts is an important part of building resilience."

"That's kind of where things went wrong!" Alicia admitted. "I lay in bed last night, stewing over what that guy said and my thoughts went super negative. But if I'm being honest, I think a part of me kind of liked getting stuck in that negativity."

"Is that a place you're familiar with?"

"What? Negativity?"

Carrie nodded.

"Oh, yeah. That's what attracted me to Brian. He could just pull me out of those negative moods and make me smile."

"Well, now you know that you can do that on your own when you pay attention to what you're thinking, and refuse to allow yourself to churn through negative thoughts. It's like you have a track in your brain that you're used to running around. It takes work to step out of those grooves and start a new track with true and positive thoughts, but the more you practice the faster you'll get at it."

"I hate running, but I do like your analogy!"

Carrie noticed the shift in the way Alicia was sitting and the tone in her voice. There was no doubt that Alicia was resilient and deter-mined to create a good life. She hoped that good life also included children but knew that part wasn't certain.

For the rest of the hour they reviewed the strategies Alicia was using to lower her stress levels, strengthen her relationship with her husband, and clarify some of the other goals in her life besides getting pregnant.

When they ended the call Alicia had successfully found the bottom of her smoothie glass, and was refocused on building healthy thoughts and words.

Carrie took a few minutes to type up her notes and send Alicia an invoice before shutting her computer down for the day. On her way out of the office, she paused briefly for a glimpse into her workshop, which was also in the basement beside the office she shared with Jonathan. It was a long ways from where she started—working at the kitchen table in a run-down townhouse trying to make enough money to buy groceries.

Now, more of her work was online orders than sales on the local buy and sell site. At the moment she was working on a custom arrangement of small brightly-colored frames all set inside a large three-foot by four-foot frame that she had rescued from beside a dumpster in the grocery store parking lot.

Jonathan teased her that she didn't need to dumpster dive anymore, but the frame was the right size and style and Carrie couldn't resist bringing it home. Her client had asked for the large frame to be painted pure white, with the phrase *Find the color inside everyone* written in black calligraphy on the bottom, and the various colorful frames arranged inside.

She continued up the stairs, through the main floor, and into the backyard where Matthew, Katie, and Maisy were enjoying the sunny spring day.

"Hi Mommy!" 8-year-old Katie shouted as soon as Carrie opened the door. Katie ran through life with great enthusiasm for everyone and everything. Today she was wearing a colorful striped skirt with built-in shorts, and a pink shirt with a sequined heart on it. Her curly brown hair was in two French braids—an attempt by Carrie to prevent some of the tangles that came with a girl who was always on the go.

At the moment Katie was hanging upside down from her knees on a bar that was part of the swing set. Carrie made a mental note to buy more skirts with shorts!

Excited to see someone else in the backyard, Maisy—the newest addition to the family—bounded over to sniff Carrie's feet. Maisy's mom had been found wandering the streets not too far from their home, and brought to the humane society where she promptly gave birth to six puppies of indiscriminate breed.

Maisy was fluffy, a mix of muted browns and greys, with adorable ears that bounced when she ran and twisted every which way to catch all the sounds in her world.

Carrie crouched down to pet Maisy, and immediately felt sharp puppy teeth clamp down on her hand. "OUCH!" she shouted as she forced her hand to go limp. Then she stood up and counted to ten before crouching down and trying to pet the puppy again.

"Good job Mommy!" Katie said, clapping. They were all trying to do everything the dog trainer had taught them, including discouraging Maisy from biting.

"Thanks." She stood up as Matthew walked over and put an arm around his shoulder. He was only about four inches shorter than her now. "I thought you'd have her fully trained by now," she teased.

"Ha ha." He looked down at his watch. "I'd better get ready for guitar lessons." With a quick kiss on her cheek he jogged inside.

Carrie felt a familiar tug on her heart. At 13, he was either super responsible or super brainless—and sometimes both within a few minutes. She knew he had a lot going on in his brain right now, but it only served to remind her that he was growing up fast and needing her a lot less than he used to. Subconsciously she put a hand on her stomach. Maybe this month…

"Mommy," Katie called as she swung back and forth, "when can I start guitar lessons?"

Carrie felt her heart twinge for a second over how fast Katie was growing. "When you give up musical theater or gymnastics."

"Can't I give up swimming?" She grabbed the bar with her hands and flipped around, landing effortlessly on her feet.

"Nope. Swimming is a life skill. Level five before you can stop swimming lessons."

Katie pouted for about a second and then smiled broadly, "At least I have lots of friends at swimming!"

"Yeah, and if you chatted a little less you'd pass your tests the first time."

"It's OK. My friends didn't pass either." She crouched to pick up a dog toy. "Maisy! Come get it!"

Carrie smiled while sending a little thought out to the current swim coach. He was young, and the three chatty girls with Katie were more than any teacher should deal with. Poor guy.

CHAPTER 2

Carrie put her feet up on the upholstered footrest in front of the master bedroom's fireplace and sighed. This had become her favorite part of the day. Whenever Jonathan wasn't traveling for work, they'd each bring a drink to their bedroom after the kids were in bed and sit together. Sometimes they read, or flipped through their phones, or just sat quietly. Most of the time they talked.

She had gotten used to not having much adult conversation in her life, but now that she had Jonathan it was clear what she had been missing. Whether they talked about the kids, their businesses, or just got to know each other better, it always left her feeling safe and fulfilled.

"So," Jonathan started as he sat down beside her on the loveseat, "Katie says she can't take guitar lessons because you're making her take swimming." Even when Carrie tucked Katie in, Jonathan loved to get a few minutes with her to say goodnight. Katie called it her 'Daddy Time'.

"Riiight. Mean old Mommy who makes her learn something that could save her life." Katie was trying hard to figure out how much she could get from her Daddy after her Mommy said no. For the most part it was a running joke between the two parents.

"Could we just start guitar on the weeks I'm home? I don't mind taking her."

"It's not going to kill her to wait a few more years. And she could move up a lot faster in swimming if she quit talking to her friends and listened to the poor instructor."

Jonathan tried not to look disappointed. He was definitely on the 'say yes as much as possible' parenting team.

Carrie chuckled at his expression. "And it's good practice for you to say no to her once in a while."

"Yeah, yeah."

Matthew knocked on the door and Carrie called for him to come in. "Maisy's crying. Can I let her out? She might have to pee."

"Sorry bud," Jonathan answered, "but she's already had a long walk and a pee when you were doing your homework. Remember, if we teach her that whining works she'll do it ten times more."

He sighed, "OK. It just makes me feel so sad when she's crying. How much longer 'til she gets used to it?"

"Well, she's doing incredibly well considering we've just had her for a few weeks. It'll be a week at the most." Jonathan smirked at Carrie. "It's good training for when you're a parent and you have to say no to your kids."

"But you don't ever say no to us!" Matthew protested innocently.

Carrie burst out laughing.

"It's my parents' fault for not having more puppies," Jonathan deadpanned before smiling. "Seriously, I *do* say no sometimes. Just tonight I told Katie she had to listen to your mom's no..." He caught Matthew's smirk. "Well, that's pretty close to saying no! Do you want to hang out with your mom and I till Maisy stops crying?"

"It's OK, I'll just play some music so I can't hear her. Night."

The both said goodnight to him, and Carrie smiled. "I thought this was supposed to be our time alone after the kids were in bed."

"Well… OK. You're right. I don't want to say no and I don't want them to ever be sad. Ever."

"Technically you said no to letting Maisy out."

He sat up straighter. "I did, didn't I? Yep, nailing this parenting thing for sure!"

She smiled at him briefly, and then her smile faded. "Speaking of parenting, how long do we try to get pregnant before we consider other options?"

"I was kinda hoping we'd never stop trying. Even when we're old. Like, really old," he winked at her. "But as far as pregnancy versus other options? I don't know. Some days I really want to have kids that are a piece of me. But most days having Matthew and Katie fills my heart so much that I just want more kids no matter where they come from."

Carrie leaned her head on his shoulder. "You are the most wonderful man."

"I am, aren't I?" They sat quietly for a few minutes, Carrie drinking her decaf tea and Jonathan drinking a hot chocolate. "What about you? What do you think we should do?"

"The hardest part for me is the emotional roller coaster. Every month I truly believe that I feel different and that I'm definitely pregnant. And then when I'm not, I'm just crushed. I think also I'm a bit like you. I want to have babies with you, but more than anything, I just want to give a few more kids lots of love and a safe home, no matter where they come from."

"We're definitely in a financial place where we can consider all the options."

"I have a client who's gone through a couple rounds of in vitro fertilization already. I really don't think that's for me. I'm not sure I can explain why. It just… I can't get excited about the thought of going through all the tests and hormone injections and appointments."

"OK… what about adoption? There are still foreign countries that accept American parents. And there are agencies here. Oh, and there's the foster system."

Carrie sighed. "Again, some days I think yes, and some days I think no. Because of my training I know a lot about the challenges kids can have when their start in life is traumatic. And we have to think about how those types of things would impact Matthew and Katie."

"I guess Lisa's experience makes fostering look so easy. Maybe easy isn't the right word. I know she's been through a lot, getting approved and everything, and then the stuff with Bethany. But it just seems like a perfect fit for her."

She nodded. Her friend Lisa had chosen to become a single foster parent, despite already being a caregiver to her mom who has rheumatoid arthritis. The first child she had been placed with was a 15-year-old pregnant girl named Bethany. Although it seemed like Bethany was settling in well at Lisa's in the first few weeks, hours after giving birth she ran away from the hospital and hadn't been heard from since. Now, Lisa was baby Marco's foster mom. He was healthy, happy, and a very good baby considering he was still less than a month old, and Lisa practically glowed whenever they visited.

Carrie sipped her tea. "But she still acknowledges Bethany as his mom, who she believes will come back any day now. *And* she thinks she'll be able to just hand Marco back to her."

"I think she was born with an exceptionally large heart. I don't know her as well as you do, of course, but she's doing a lot of things a typical 26-year-old would never do."

"And," she reminded him, "there are not a lot of healthy babies in the foster system. So many are born with drug and alcohol dependencies, not to mention brain damage and physical problems."

"But you said studies show that most drug babies can thrive with a good environment. That the drug exposure doesn't seem to do long-term damage."

"I didn't know you were listening when I talked to Matthew about that."

"I was. Another epic parenting moment by you I might add."

"Thanks." She paused. "I swear though, some days the only point of my psychology degree is to be able to answer more of Matthew's questions. That kid ponders social issues like most boys ponder video games."

"Hey, he is definitely catching up in the video game area. Beat the pants off me the other day when we were playing."

"Should I ask him to go easy on you? Technically you're still a new dad. That might be too harsh for the first few years, getting smoked by a kid."

"Well, I'm such an awesome husband it probably helps that I have a few very tiny areas where I'm not perfect."

"You joke, but you're right. And sometimes I feel like there are some kids out there who need to have an awesome dad like you in their life."

Jonathan cleared his throat and finished his hot chocolate. "Are you finished with your tea? I can take our mugs down."

"Yeah, thanks." She watched him go downstairs, knowing he needed a moment alone. After six months, she could tell when he was suddenly missing his own dad. It was a grief she couldn't do anything about, except hope that with enough joy in his life the pain would ease.

They had taken Matthew and Katie to the cemetery to leave flowers on Jonathan's parents' graves at Christmas, and together with Jenny, Carrie was working on a scrapbook for their kids so they would know about the grandparents they'd never get to meet in person. Jenny's daughter Angela was Katie's age, and had been a baby when her grandparents died so she didn't have any memories either.

CHAPTER 3

"Matthew? Matthew!" Carrie called. "It's time to go!"

"What? How?"

Carrie resisted the urge to roll her eyes. It seemed like the more his body grew the less his brain was willing to keep up. He was supposed to wake up and get ready for school independently and Carrie was trying to let him succeed or fail on his own. But after listening to him fiddle on his guitar for the last twenty minutes she was pretty sure he had forgotten about time.

He ran downstairs a minute later, his backpack dangling from one arm. Carrie walked back up the stairs and picked up the water bottle and cell phone that had fallen out, put them back in his backpack, and zipped it up while he shoved his feet inside his sneakers.

"Do you have a lunch?"

"No, I forgot."

Jonathan walked over from the kitchen carrying a paper bag. "It's your lucky day. I was practicing my lunch making skills."

Matthew gave him a grateful look, shoved the lunch in his backpack, and yelled, "Thanks Dad! Bye Mom!" as he ran out to the side of the house where his bike was locked up.

Jonathan beamed. "I got my first 'Dad'! Woohoo!" He held his hand up for a high five and Carrie obliged.

"And I'm sure it had nothing to do with making lunch for a kid who's perfectly capable of doing it the night before like I taught him."

"Hey, that very healthy lunch might be just the thing he needs to get that brain of his firing again."

Carrie snorted. "Not likely! We've probably got six months to a year of this before we get lulled into thinking his frontal lobe has actually made some connections, and then he'll fall back into even more brainlessness."

"At least we'll get a break in between."

"Fingers crossed." She checked her phone. "I'd better get Katie going."

"Right. Your coffee morning with Jenny."

"I'm looking forward to it. At least when I was her housecleaner I got to chat with her twice a week. Now that we're sisters and both working it seems like we never get a chance to catch up."

"Say hi to her for me." He went into the kitchen where Katie was sitting on a stool at the island and slowly working through a piece of toast. "I'm heading downstairs to work. You have a good day, OK?"

Katie reached her arms up for a hug, and he hugged her for a good minute before she let go. "Bye Daddy. I love you!"

"I love you too!" He stopped at Carrie for a good-bye kiss before going downstairs to their office.

"Alright. Finish eating and brush your teeth. We need to be out the door in five minutes."

"I wish you could drive me every day." Normally Carrie or Jonathan

—or both—walked Katie the fifteen minutes to school and they were out the door before Matthew.

"I *can* drive you every day, but walking is good exercise. It's good for Maisy, too."

"Can Maisy come in the car?"

"Nope. I'm going to Aunty Jenny's for coffee after I drop you off and I don't want to deal with Maisy."

Katie jumped off her stool and went to put her plate in the dishwasher. "Aw, poor Maisy has to go in her crate!"

Carrie picked up a doggy treat and walked over to the crate. "Yeah poor Maisy gets a treat and a nap. Sounds pretty good to me!" She gave the dog the treat and Maisy eagerly took it and went into her crate to start chewing it.

Five minutes later Carrie was creeping forward in the school drop off lane. "We need an electric car like Lisa so we're not putting pollution in the air."

"I don't like Lisa's car," Katie said from the back seat.

"Why not?"

"It's too quiet. I never know whether it's going or not."

"It must be nice to ride in such a quiet car though."

Katie shrugged. When they got to the stop point an older student opened her door and she climbed out. "Bye! Have fun drinking coffee!"

Carrie slowly pulled away, smiling. Katie always managed to make everyone around her smile.

When she pulled up in front of Jenny's house she got out quickly and ran up the stairs and into the house. "I'm here!" she called up as she took off her shoes and hung up her coat.

"Coffee's waiting for you!" Jenny called back.

Carrie ran up the stairs and took a minute to appreciate how good Jenny looked. When they first met three years ago Jenny was in the worst part of cancer treatments. She had been so thin Carrie was afraid of breaking her when she helped her get around the house, and her voice had been weak and shaky.

Now, Jenny was vibrant and glowing. She had put on over twenty pounds, her cheeks were no longer hollow, and her straight brown hair looked thick and healthy in an asymmetrical bob.

"Hey, I love the hair! Wow, you can really pull it off. You're practically glowing!" she hugged her recently acquired sister-in-law and then pulled back. "Wait a minute … is that a special kind of glow?"

Jenny's entire face lit up.

"Jenny! For real?"

Jenny nodded. "Officially five weeks pregnant. Hope you're ready for extra aunty duties!"

For a moment Carrie felt a pang of sadness and maybe even jealousy. They had talked about getting pregnant together, but it was silly for Jenny to wait. And it was miraculous that she was able to get pregnant after all she'd been through.

"Of course I'm ready. And I'm so happy for you!"

The both sat down at the table where Jenny already had Carrie's coffee ready for her. Carrie leaned forward and looked into Jenny's mug, "That looks pretty weak for tea."

"Yeah, there's some sites that say herbal teas are bad for baby so I've switched to hot water and lemon in the mornings."

"Seriously? Herbal tea? I thought it was bad enough when they said no coffee during pregnancy!"

"Well, I'd say we're going way overboard on the caution, but I want to do everything I can to have a full-term, healthy baby."

"What else are you doing?" Carrie couldn't think of anything else to add. Jenny and Max lived a pretty healthy lifestyle already.

Jenny laughed. "Maybe it's easier to say what we're *not* doing. Let's see, entire house is chemical free. Entire fridge and cupboards are organic—although I did draw the line when Max wanted me to switch to only wearing organic cotton clothes. And we've got this new ridiculously expensive water filtration system. I have to admit though, when we eat out now I definitely notice the taste in water."

"And what about Angela? Have you told her?"

"We'll wait until I start to show before we tell her. She's so sensitive. I want to be careful about any new changes. And I'll feel more comfortable telling her when I'm past the first trimester."

"Let me know what you need for help. Is the housekeeper still working out?" Carrie knew that Jenny need a calm, clean, and organized house but was helpless at doing it herself. She joked that Katie got her hurricane-like tendencies from her Auntie Jenny.

"Carrie, I don't need you to come and clean my house thank you very much. Although nobody's come close to how good you were. But I would really like it if we figured out a way to spend more time together. I feel a little bit lost without your listening ear and wise answers every week."

"I'd love that. And since we both technically control our own schedules, there's no actual reason to go so long without visits. Texting isn't exactly the same as this," she said, gesturing to her and Jenny.

"So, that's my big news. What about you guys?"

"Not much to say. Oh, that's not true! Matthew yelled 'thanks Dad' to Jonathan today on his way out the door.

Jenny's eyes filled with tears. "Jonathan got his first 'Dad' from Matthew?"

Carrie nodded. "It definitely made his day. I mean, Katie's been calling him Daddy since the second we got engaged, but Matthew needed to do it in his own time."

"My gosh. A year ago you weren't even engaged yet. And here you are an old married couple now!"

"Yeah, I was just thinking back to this time last year when I was scrambling to get all my assignments handed in in time to graduate with my Masters. I really had no idea that I'd be here a year later."

"And what about the baby front for you two?" Jenny caressed her stomach. "This little one wants lots of cousins."

Carrie looked down for a moment. "Still nothing. I know we haven't been trying that long, but every month is such a disappointment. We're starting to talk about alternatives. Maybe adopting."

"Any kids you get, in any way, will be lucky to have you two as parents."

"Thanks! Have you told *your* parents?"

"Oh, I'm glad you mentioned that. Nope, just you. And Max is going to ask Jonathan out for a beer tonight and tell him and then you two have to keep quiet about it. We just couldn't keep this to ourselves, but I want to wait until we're further along to tell anyone else."

"They are going to flip out!"

"Totally. You know, with you guys and us here we'd really like them to move closer. I know they've got their precious cottage and all their friends there, but a four hour flight is just too far away when you've got little grandkids."

"It would be amazing to have them close by." Carrie smirked. "Maybe they're afraid if they move here we'll all just book them up for babysitting and they won't have a life anymore."

"Good point. We won't tell them about that part until they're here for good!"

"Deal!" Carrie said, and held up her mug to Jenny's. Getting a sister-in-law, brother-in-law, niece, and 'borrowed' parents-in-law when she married Jonathan was extra special and she knew how fortunate she was. Jenny's parents had immediately taken Jonathan under their wing when his and Max's parents had died in a car accident, and they considered Carrie and the kids part of their family too.

CHAPTER 4

"Hey, does it work if Max and I go out for a beer tonight?" Jonathan asked at dinner.

"Of course! It's been a while since you guys had a brother's night out." Carrie answered and tilted her head towards Matthew. His shoulders hunched up and he clenched his glass of milk. The memories of his dad coming home drunk were hopefully fading, but he still didn't like the thought of adults drinking.

"I'm going to walk over to that pub by our pizza place, and then Max and I will share an Uber home," Jonathan said casually. "It's been a while since we shot the breeze together."

"Beer's stinky," Katie piped up.

"I'll keep that in mind Katie. Don't worry, I won't bring anything stinky home."

"Mom, do you think I can go to camp this summer?" Matthew asked.

The quick shift in conversation took Carrie off guard.

"Definitely," Jonathan answered. "What did you have in mind?"

"My guitar teacher said at lessons last night that there was a music camp I should consider. I forgot to give you the flyer, hang on." He got up and ran up to his room, coming back shortly with a flyer.

Carrie opened it up to see the cost and nearly choked on her chicken fettuccini alfredo. "I don't think —"

"—Your mom doesn't think she can be away from you for more than two days," Jonathan interrupted, "but Katie and I will keep her so busy she'll only miss you a little bit. Right Katie?"

"Right!"

Matthew proceeded to tell them everything about the camp, getting more excited the more he talked about it.

Katie wiggled in her chair until Matthew finished talking, "Mommy, can I go to summer camp too?"

"You can do Vacation Bible School, and gymnastics camp, and YMCA camp." Carrie said. Those camps were now looking like a bargain compared to what Matthew's would cost. She wondered if he could get a part-time job to help pay for it.

"But I want to go to sleepover camp!" Katie protested.

"Let's see how your mom handles Matthew being away. We don't want her to be too sad, right?"

Katie gave Jonathan a suspicious look. "You can make her happy for both of us. And there's Maisy!"

Later that evening Carrie tried to concentrate on the novel she was reading, but her mind kept wandering to how expensive Matthew's camp was and how Jonathan was feeling about Max and Jenny expecting.

When he came in at 10:30 she realized she hadn't even turned a page in the past half an hour.

"Hey gorgeous," he said kissing her head. "I'm just going to brush my teeth and say hi to Matthew."

"He should be sleeping."

"If he is, he's sleeping with his light on."

Fifteen minutes later Jonathan came and joined her on the loveseat in their bedroom. "Man," he said quietly, "he was so stressed that I'd be drunk. You'd think by now he'd know that I'm different than Don in every way." He ran his hands through his hair and leaned his head back.

"Those old memories are connected to a lot of fear so they're still more powerful than logic for him. I'll talk to him about it in a day or so. But all you can do is keep showing him how different things are now. The fact that he's calling you Dad now, and loves spending time with you says a lot about how much he trusts you."

"You're right. But it's hard not to take it personally."

Carrie gave him a sympathetic smile. "I know. How was your night?"

"It's always good to hang out with Max."

"And … did he have any news?"

"Oh, about Jenny. Yeah. He's totally freaked out."

"What? I thought he'd be super excited. They've wanted to have more kids for a while now."

"We talked a lot about that. He said now that she's pregnant, it's different. He's terrified something's going to happen to her. Did you know women still die in childbirth here? And they can get things like massive strokes that leave them brain dead or paralyzed? And because she's over thirty she's got a way higher risk of complications? And—"

Carrie put a hand on his chest. "Whoa there Tex. Ease up on the stampede of terror. Yes, those are all possible. But they're very, *very* small risks. Jenny's going to be just fine! Although that does explain some of the things they're doing. Did you know he wanted her to switch to wearing only organic clothes?"

"Is that even a thing? No, I didn't know that. He just said they were going to do everything right and not take any risks. Good thing she works from home or he'd probably try to make her quit her job."

Carrie shook her head. "There's no way she'd agree to that. It was hard enough for her to take a break from her clients when she was getting treatments." Jenny was a financial advisor who met with clients all around the world in virtual meetings from her home office. Her work set-up had been the inspiration for Carrie to start her counseling business from home.

"So, Jenny's happy?"

"Jenny's literally glowing with happiness. If she has the same fears Max has, she's hiding them pretty well."

"And how are you with all of this?"

"I was going to ask you the same thing. I definitely had to get over a pang of jealousy. But I'm really happy for them. And for us! We're literally doubling our niece or nephew count in one go! And the kids will be so excited to have another cousin."

"Yeah, that part's pretty cool. I just ... all the stuff Max said about pregnancy. It's a lot to take in."

"Hey, women have been doing the whole pregnancy and baby thing since the beginning of time. This isn't anything new."

He reached and pulled her into his arms. "Yeah, but for me it's completely new and totally terrifying."

CHAPTER 5

Carrie settled into her chair and adjusted her earbuds. Two virtual client sessions were complete, and Alicia would be her last session of the day. Jonathan was driving Matthew to his friend's and then taking Katie swimming because it was raining too hard to play outside, and Carrie was looking forward to a quiet house for a bit after her session.

She paused to look around their basement office. What a change from the dark, dingy basement she used to avoid when she was living in subsidized housing as a single mom! Knowing they would each spend hours every day there, her husband had insisted on putting in heated floors and a large two-person desk, along with floor-to-ceiling shelves that had more than enough room for books and memorabilia. The walls were a warm white, and the windows at the top of the walls let in a surprising amount of natural light.

Carrie loved her work as a counseling psychologist, and her current schedule was just about perfect. Three days a week she had virtual sessions from home. That left one day to work at the clinic where Kara, one of her best friends, was a physician's assistant, and one day to work on her business upcycling picture frames. If she needed, she could always do some work on the weekends around whatever activities the kids happened to have.

She only had to wait a second for the connection to pop up with Alicia, but one look and it was clear something was wrong. She was crying and held a finger up to pause Carrie while she worked to get her emotions under control. After a few minutes she took a shuddering breath. "Sorry Carrie. It's been the worst day …"

"Hey, take your time. When you're ready you can say whatever you want."

She gave a bitter smile. "I *want* to say that I'm pregnant and we're both delighted. My reality is that Brian told me this morning he's not sure this is what he wants."

"This as in a baby?"

"Well, more like this as in him and I." She started crying again.

Carrie knew they had been together since university and had shared a rather adventurous life in the past. But her sessions with Alicia had been about infertility. The relationship had come up in conversation but only in the context of supporting each other.

"Wow. Alicia I'm so sorry. This is brutal news."

Alicia nodded and wiped away her tears. "My first thought was that if I was pregnant I'd be OK because I'd still have a baby. And then my second thought was that I was so glad I wasn't pregnant because I don't want to do that alone."

"I know that infertility can be really hard on a relationship. Is that the case here?"

"Well, a lot of our discussions for the past year have been about me, my cycles, my hormones … I kinda thought since all he had to do was have a little fun alone in the doctor's office that he wouldn't have any issues …"

"You've been though a lot physically and emotionally."

"Yeah. So much. But I thought I was doing it all for us, and for our future together. Actually, I felt like I was really taking one for the team, you know?"

"I can see that."

"I was so shocked this morning I didn't really handle it very well. My gosh, Carrie. Between the IVF treatments and how messed up I've been, maybe he just couldn't stand to be around my bawling all the time."

"There's a lot we can unpack here. But I think it boils down to one question. What will *you* do *now*?" Carrie asked gently.

"This is all that choices stuff, isn't it?" She didn't wait for Carrie to answer. "I can't even think. I called in sick to work. They're used to it now because of the treatments. And I probably sounded like crap over the phone. I thought about throwing Brian's beer fridge in the dumpster next door—they're renovating. And I thought about pretending I was sick and dying so Brian would come back to me. Honestly, that's all I've got."

"Both those thoughts involve getting something from Brian. It's understandable, but not effective. What will you do for you? Let's narrow the focus. What will you do for you during the next hour after we finish our session?"

"Cry. Just cry."

"OK. And then what?" Carrie was trying to judge how to empower Alicia without overwhelming her. It was a hard place to find. She scribbled a dollar sign onto the notepad she kept beside the computer during sessions. If Brian really was leaving Alicia, she may need to take some important financial steps to try to protect herself.

"Uh ... Brian said he'd be at his friends for a few days... he does the cooking so if I want to eat I'll have to call for takeout. But I'm not hungry ..." She looked around, as if the answer was in the room somewhere.

"Have you told anyone else beside me?"

"God no. I'd be so embarrassed. We're the ones who have it all together. Dated in university, travelled a ton, paid off our student loans and bought a house before having kids. I've … um … I kinda thought I was better than some of our friends and family. Now? To be like, hey, we just blew tons of money trying to get pregnant but it's a good thing it didn't work because now we're splitting up."

She started crying again and Carrie waited patiently for a minute.

"OK, I'm going to give you a little task for after your hour of crying." Carrie was relieved to see Alicia smile through her tears. "I want you to do a little bit of writing. Every sentence needs to start with the phrase 'I choose' and then I want you to write what you choose to think, what you choose to say, and what you choose to do for the rest of the day. It can be one sentence for each thing, or it might be a lot more. That's OK. And then I want you to email me your choices."

"So, I'm guessing 'I choose to keep crying' isn't an option?"

"Actually, it is. You choose whatever you want. I'm not here to judge you or correct you or anything like that. I'm here to listen to you and support you."

"Thanks Carrie. I don't know what I'd do without you."

"Alicia, whatever comes next in your life will have its challenges, but I can tell you what I've seen over and over again. Women are amazing. *You* are amazing. We get knocked down so many times in so many different ways, but we get up, we brush ourselves off, sometimes we reinvent ourselves, and then we keep going."

"I've never really thought of myself as strong."

"I disagree. You connect very deeply with the word resilient. You are already strong and resilient. It's just been hard for you to see it in yourself."

Carrie took a calming breath. She knew the next things she'd say would either empower Alicia or terrify her. "Now I want to talk a little bit about some very practical things. Well, one thing in particular, which is finances. Are you set up to have your own income and expenses separate from your joint accounts?"

"Not really. I mean, we both make really good money, so we pool our paychecks to cover things like the mortgage and everything, and then we usually each take out what we want to spend."

"Do you have a bank account that's only in your name?"

"Yeah, I've had the same one since I was a teenager. I never use it, but I never closed it or anything."

"OK. I want you to seriously consider moving your deposit for your paychecks into your own account, and perhaps a portion of the money in your joint account that isn't earmarked for expenses."

Alicia was quiet.

"Tell me what you're thinking," Carrie said gently.

"Maybe money's part of it. He said this morning that he could've bought that boat he wanted with all the money we've spent on IVF. When he mentioned buying a boat last year, I honestly thought he was joking." She rubbed her hands across her forehead, "I think I even laughed. Oh my God. What if he's mad that we spent money on me getting pregnant when all he wanted was a boat?"

"I think that's a discussion for another day. The financial steps may not be necessary, but very often when there's a relationship break-down—even a temporary one—the woman suffers a much bigger financial impact. When it comes to money, focus on making practical and fair decisions, but ones that give you control over your earnings."

Alicia nodded. "When my sister's husband left he maxed their joint credit card and she was pretty screwed. Plus she only worked part time. At least I've got a good job."

Carrie silently agreed. Alicia was already in a much better position than many women who had limited earning potential.

"If you decide to take some financial steps when will you take them?"

"Honestly? I think I'm going to do it right away. Writing all those 'I choose' statements might make me super emotional again and I might not be up for it then."

"OK, I think that's a sound decision. We have our next session scheduled in a week. Does that work for you or would you like to add something in before then?"

"Can you fit me in at all tomorrow?" Alicia chewed her lip. I feel like I'm gonna need to talk to someone again soon. Then maybe I'll be OK until our regular time."

Carrie pulled up her online booking system. "Yep, I can do the same time tomorrow. And that way if you go to work you can still fit it in." She knew that Alicia worked early in the morning and was always home by three.

"OK. Thanks again Carrie. And hey, at the end here I made it at least five minutes without sobbing."

"See? Resilient. That's what you are."

After the call ended and Carrie typed her notes and sent the invoice, she sat back in her chair. While the end of her first marriage had been her choice, the financial fall-out had landed hard on her own shoulders. She paid off the last of those debts before she married Jonathan, but she made a lot of sacrifices to do so. Somedays it seemed like the universe was designed to always make women pay the price.

CHAPTER 6

A day later, and after another session with Alicia, Carrie walked into the kitchen and sighed. There was a time when she told Matthew to leave a dirty mug on the counter once in a while, just to try and make him relax a little. Well, he was definitely relaxed now. By the look of it, he had made a grilled cheese sandwich for an after school snack. The dirty pan was on the stove, there were cheese wrappers on the counter, the butter was out, and there were crumbs and butter smeared on the side of the stove.

Her session with Alicia had gone as well as could be expected for someone trying to come to grips with a life-changing situation, and she felt drained. The last thing she wanted to do was parent.

She walked upstairs to Matthew's room where he was lying on the floor with his guitar propped on his bent legs, headphones on, playing along to a song that sounded almost familiar. Part of a grilled cheese sandwich was on a plate on his bed. Maisy was on the floor beside him, her tail wagging.

"Hey bud? Matthew?" She walked into his room and tapped him on the shoulder.

He pulled one headphone back. "Hey Mom."

"Hey you. I see you made a grilled cheese sandwich."

"Three! But I got a little full after two and a half. You want it?"

"No thanks. Can you go clean up the kitchen? You left a mess."

"Oh, I forgot. Yeah. C'mon Maisy!"

Carrie stopped him and pointed to the bed. "What's the rule?"

"Oh yeah, I forgot." He grabbed the plate and went downstairs with Maisy at his heels. Carrie decided to ignore the mess in his room for now. At least the kitchen would be cleaner when he was done.

The quiet house filled with life when Jonathan and Katie came in the door. "Guess what? I listened to the swim guy today for the WHOLE time! Daddy said I did really really good!"

"What, the one time I'm not there you decide to listen?"

"Don't take it personally," Jonathan said as he bent to untie his shoes. "Two of her friends were missing today."

"But I still listened really good!" Katie insisted.

"Yes, you did," Jonathan said smiling. "Go wash your hands and hang up your swimsuit and towel, OK?"

"OK Daddy!" she said and ran into the bathroom. They could hear her singing at the top of her lungs as she splashed water.

"Hey," Jonathan said, leaning over to kiss her. "How was the session?"

"Hard. I'm pretty drained. Thanks for taking Katie to swim lessons for me. My client thinks she'll be fine until our regular scheduled session next week now."

"No problem. It's a good thing I went so she behaved," he added with a wink.

Carrie made her way to the kitchen where a pork roast had been in the crockpot since the morning. She pulled it apart, leaving the shredded meat to sit in the juices while she heated up a can of beans, tossed a salad, and cut buns for pulled pork sandwiches.

She had to check the family schedule because she couldn't remember who was on table setting and cleaning up.

"Katie!" she called. "Come set the table and then we can eat!"

Katie was much more enthusiastic about supper duties now that it included feeding Maisy. Carrie watched out of the corner of her eye as Katie carefully measured out the food, stepped away, and waited a few seconds before giving Maisy permission to eat. It seemed like the dog thrived on having rules to follow, and she was always eager to listen for their commands.

As they sat eating a few minutes later, Carrie couldn't help but feel lucky. She had a faithful, loving husband, two healthy kids, they were eating well, and buying groceries hadn't left her in tears. She wondered how Alicia was doing, alone in the house she had shared with her husband.

"Mommy," Katie interrupted her thoughts.

"Mmmmhmmm?"

"Why isn't a baby in your tummy?"

Jonathan snorted into his drink, and Carrie resisted the urge to tell Katie to ask her Daddy.

"It's not always something we can control. Sometimes babies grow in mommies tummies and sometimes they don't." She hoped Katie wouldn't ask more about where babies came from. One look at Matthew and she figured he was thinking the same thing.

"Oh." Katie took a spoonful of beans, chewed, and swallowed. "I thought when you married Daddy I'd get a sister or a brother. Can I still have one?" Her eyebrows furrowed. "Is your tummy broken?"

"No, my tummy isn't broken. And families don't always come from the mommy's tummy."

"I KNOW! Daddy didn't come from your tummy!"

Now it was Matthew's turn to spit out his drink.

"And thank goodness for that," Carrie answered dryly.

"Where else do babies come from?"

"Uh, well Lisa's baby didn't come from her tummy. What Lisa's doing is like adopting a baby. She's a mommy to Marcus even though he didn't grow in her tummy."

"Will Bethany have more babies and give them to Lisa? Marcus will need a little brother or sister."

Carrie gave Jonathan a pointed look. It was his turn to answer a few impossible questions.

"Well," he said slowly, "maybe when Marcus is a bit older there will be another boy or girl who needs Lisa to be their mommy too. Every little boy and girl needs a mommy, don't you think so?"

Tears immediately pooled in Katies eyes. "There are boys and girls with no mommies?"

"Uh, well, maybe, uh, they have daddies?"

"Well I had a daddy and a mommy, and then my daddy was bad but I still had a mommy and then I got a daddy *Johnny* and now I have a daddy and a mommy for forever. Why can't the other boys and girls have a daddy and a mommy for forever? It's not fair!" she wailed.

Jonathan slid back his chair. "Come here Katie-girl." She immediately left her chair and climbed into his lap, snuggling into his chest as he wrapped his arms around her.

Carrie felt her heart clench with sadness. She knew there were boys and girls without mommies and daddies. Maybe even ones that went to her children's school. Katie was right. Every child should have a daddy's lap to crawl into when they were sad.

"Katie, there are some really sad things in the world," Jonathan said quietly. "Boys and girls without daddies and mommies is *very* sad." He cleared his throat and blinked a few times. "Sometimes we can do something to make some of the sad things go away. And sometimes there's nothing we can do except pray for them. But all the time I am right here to be your Daddy. And that's a happy thing, right?"

Katie nodded her head. After a few minutes Jonathan slid her plate over and she finished her supper while sitting on his lap. She was unusually quiet as she cleaned up supper.

After she was in bed, Carrie and Jonathan sat in the living room. There was some sort of home renovation show on, but neither one of them was really watching it. When Matthew came in from taking Maisy for her night walk he joined them.

"You know that stuff you were talking to Katie about? Like, boys and girls who don't have parents?"

They nodded.

"Well, I was thinking. Like, babies are great and all. But, there are kids already alive who are alone. Or maybe they're in a crappy foster home like the one Bethany was in before she came to Lisa's. And we're … like, you guys are OK parents. And we're not broke. Like, we have money for more food and stuff if we wanted … I just thought. Maybe some of those kids need us. You know?"

Carrie heard Jonathan sigh deeply. "That's pretty much what I've been thinking about since supper. You know, I don't need any more kids to be happy. You and Katie are everything and enough. But now that I'm your dad I feel like my heart's bigger than it used to be."

Matthew's eyes lit up. "You mean, like loving us gives you room to love more kids?"

"Maybe. I don't know for sure. I guess your mom and I have a lot of talking and thinking to do. But I have to say, you coming to us and the things you've just said kind of make me want to explode with pride that you're my son."

CHAPTER 7

Carrie lay in bed cuddled into Jonathan. He absentmindedly stroked her hair.

"You can always trust Katie to drop a bombshell when you least expect it."

He chuckled. "Yeah, I was so focused on hoping she wouldn't ask where babies come from that I didn't see all that daddy and mommy stuff coming."

"You're really good with her."

"What I really wanted was to just run out in the street and grab all the kids without parents and bring them home. Holding her in my lap didn't just make *her* feel better."

"She has a point. About kids out there that could use a family."

"Well, Matthew did say we're OK parents. Does that count on an adoption application?"

Now it was Carrie's turn to chuckle. "If he wasn't so serious right then I would've teased him about that. But what about fostering?

There are a lot of kids in the foster system. Just think about how overworked Lisa's social worker is."

They were quiet for a while.

"I don't think I can do that Carrie."

"What?"

"Foster. I can't … the thought of having some kid in our home who came from a bad place, and then having to let them go back to that. That would kill me."

"Yeah. Every time Lisa talks about Bethany coming back or she talks to Marcus about his mommy I kind want to, well, I don't know. I just don't understand how she can be so loving about it. I mean, Bethany abandoned her baby, but she doesn't seem to ever think about that."

"I don't think we should even try to be like Lisa. She's on a whole different level with what she's doing."

"Mmmhmmm," Carrie agreed.

"So … what about adoption?"

"I don't know. You know, some of those kids come with some pretty major needs. Things I couldn't deal with."

He took a deep breath and let it out slowly. "I'm not sure I want to know. What do you mean?"

"Well, if they've experienced abuse of any kind then their understanding of love and relationships is going to be challenging. They might resist genuine love for a long time, or they may try to abuse us or Matthew and Katie and Maisy because it's what they've been taught."

"Oh. But it kinda makes me want to love those kids anyways and put their parents in jail."

"That's part of it too," Carrie continued. "Whatever they've been through, we'll kind of go through it too as their parents. I read one case study in school about an adoptive mom who had some pretty major mental health issues when her daughter told her about all the abuse she had experienced in her birth parent's home."

"Don't you think we—well, especially you—would be better equipped to handle that? With your training and your experience?"

"I'd still have to make my way through all the feelings and my own reactions. And so would you, and you have a pretty soft heart."

"Is that all? I mean, are those all the challenges that come with adopting?"

"I'm not an expert or anything. If we're serious about this we need to do a lot more research. But there's the drug and alcohol exposure. I know we talked about it a little bit the other day. One of the reasons I chose to focus on working with adults is because I couldn't deal with the challenges kids with fetal alcohol syndrome have. It breaks my heart—they literally have gaps in their brains. Whatever was developing when their mom was drinking can be completely gone."

"I don't want us to consider anything that we can't handle. We are lucky to have two amazing kids. And having Matthew call me Dad the other day. That was … it was like the best thing ever."

"Except for marrying me," Carrie reminded him.

He kissed her forehead. "Definitely second after marrying you."

The next day as Carrie worked in the room they called her studio, she replayed her conversation from the night before, and Katie's words at dinner time. Were they meant to adopt? What if the kid hated them? Or hated Matthew and Katie? She couldn't imagine her kids hating anyone, but she knew that sometimes it only took one difficult child to tear apart an entire family.

As she covered a variety of frames in white primer, she tried to weigh the pros and cons in her head. Although Lisa was her only friend who had experience as a sort-of adoptive mom, she didn't feel like she could talk to her and get a balanced answer. Lisa was loving every second of raising Marcus—even though she had never planned on having a newborn.

There *was* Lisa's social worker, Mark. Maybe she and Jonathan could set up a meeting with him. She had a feeling this was an idea that wasn't going to go away. All they could do at this point was to get more information so they could make the best decision for their future and their family.

Satisfied with her conclusion, she walked over to the office where Jonathan was working. He looked up from the computer screen.

"Hey, is it lunch already?" They tried to always eat lunch together when they were both working from home.

"No. I just wanted to run something by you. What do you think about inviting Lisa's social worker Mark to meet us for coffee? Maybe he could answer some of our questions, and point us in the right direction."

His shoulders sagged with relief. "That's a great idea. I've been trying to concentrate all morning without much luck. Taking action —even just setting up a meeting with Mark—might help me put all this to the side for now so I can get some work done."

She put her arm around him and kissed his cheek. "OK. I'll get his number and set something up. Now hopefully you can get some work done."

A notification popped up on his screen and he nodded in response. Carrie smiled as she left the room. She knew if he got wrapped up in his work he would actually forget everything else for a bit. Considering the big decisions they might have to make, a little bit of forgetting would be a nice break.

CHAPTER 8

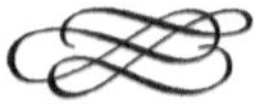

"Hey you guys!" Mark hurried over to the table Carrie and Jonathan had been sitting at for almost ten minutes. "I'm so sorry to keep you waiting. I seem to always be at least an hour behind these days."

"Well, in that case you're early!" Carrie quipped.

"What can we get you to drink?" Jonathan asked. "Our treat."

"The largest thing with the most caffeine please."

"Got it," Jonathan said with a laugh as he stood up and went to the counter to order.

"That busy, huh?"

Mark slumped in his chair and put his hands in his pockets. "Yeah. I keep on trying to save every kid. You'd think I'd learn by now, but I always want to give them one more chance. You know, just maybe the next foster home will work. Or maybe a different school. I even try to set them up with different social workers so they don't have to deal with me against their will."

"Wow. Time for a lecture on letting go coupled with a good dose of self-care maybe?"

He gave a half-smile. "I always say after this kid I'll ease off. But there's always another kid waiting. But enough about my problems. We don't have time for all that. What did you guys want to see me about?"

Jonathan rejoined them. "Well, Carrie and I were wondering if you could tell us a bit about adopting kids that are in the foster system."

"Dang. I was hoping you'd want to become foster parents."

"I know it's a huge need, but I couldn't let a kid go. Especially if I knew they were going back to a bad place."

"That's the worst part, for sure. OK. I can respect that. I don't do adoptions. When I get any of my kids into full government custody they're assigned an adoption worker who takes over."

"How long does it take to get custody of them?" Jonathan asked.

He blew out a breath, sat up, and leaned forward with his elbows on the table and his hands crossed. Jonathan held up a hand, and got up and brought their coffees back.

Mark nodded his thanks and took a sip of his coffee. "Perfect coffee, thank you. So, custody depends on a lot of things. I mean, the ultimate goal is to keep families together. That's really more my focus. Working with the parents when I can, keeping sibling groups together, trying to find other family that can help or even take the kids in. To be granted custody we have to prove that none of those things were effective. Even in a case like Bethany and baby Marcus, we'll wait as long as possible to see if she comes back before seeking custody."

"Wow, man. I don't know how you do this job."

He looked at Jonathan and smiled. "That part's easy. I'm here. I'm doing what I can. It's never enough but it's better than doing nothing. And sometimes we save a kid, or even a whole family that wouldn't have survived without us. It's all worth it on those days."

Jonathan took Carrie's hand. "Maybe that's what we're looking for. The chance to make a difference somewhere, rather than doing nothing."

Mark nodded. "I totally get that. So. Adoption. From my point of view, every child up for adoption is a special needs child because they've been separated from their birth parents. That means you've got to learn more, work harder, be more patient, and be more willing to learn from your mistakes than the average parent."

"Oh," he continued, "I should start a little earlier. The adoption application is pretty intense. You're going to have a huge stack of questionnaires each, a couple of interviews, home visits, interviews with your kids, credit checks, income verification, blood tests—"

"—blood tests?" Carrie asked.

He shrugged. "Don't ask me why, but it's a thing here. Give yourself three or four months from start until approval. And then the child selling begins."

"Excuse me?" Jonathan looked shocked. So did Carrie.

"The thing is, there's a lot more kids waiting for forever homes than homes waiting for kids. In our city alone there's about fourteen hundred kids waiting for families. So adoption workers do their darndest to get those kids in homes. They try to be honest with you about each child, but they definitely want to sell you on the one they think is the best fit for you. No matter how badly you want to help every child, you need to rule by your head, not your heart."

"Wow. OK. This whole conversation is messing with my head right now," Jonathan admitted.

"Sorry. It's my normal so it's easy to forget that you two are hearing this for the first time."

"Why haven't you and your wife adopted?" Carrie asked.

"At this point, that's a head thing. We know we can do more through our agency for more kids if we don't have kids of our own."

"Geez, you're as amazing—or as crazy—as Lisa."

"Yeah, she's definitely a success story. Which makes Marcus a success story."

"How do you deal with Bethany, and what happened there?"

"That's another important thing for adoptive parents to consider, actually."

Carrie leaned forward. "How's that?"

He finished his coffee and looked disappointed. "Bethany's mom is an alcoholic. Before Bethany was apprehended at eleven years old she lived in constant chaos and uncertainty. They were frequently homeless, Bethany nursed her mom and probably saved her life numerous times when she was binge drinking, and who knows what or who she was exposed to in those conditions."

"But, Bethany always maintained a powerful connection to her mom. It's something that's quite common. No matter how bad life is, these kids love their parents, are incredibly loyal to them, and will even be so overwhelmed with guilt if they end up in a safe foster home that they do everything they can to get back to the home environment they're familiar with."

"So, I expect that Bethany left to be with her mom. From my point of view, the fact that she had excellent prenatal care, along with love and safety, for the few months she was with Lisa *and* she waited until Marcus was born before she left, are all signs that the system is working. Marcus already has a better chance than his mom or his grandma."

Jonathan took Carrie's hand. "I've always thought what you were doing was amazing. But now? Dude, you're a hero. I don't know where we fit in with all of this. I'm more scared, and yet more compelled to do what we can."

"Well," Mark held up his coffee cup, "aside from providing me with some much-needed caffeine, I really appreciate you listening. The more people that understand what these kids, and us social workers, and all parents are facing, the better."

They said their good-byes, and Jonathan and Carrie held hands while they drove home. Both were silent and lost in their thoughts.

CHAPTER 9

"Mom?"

Carrie looked up from her laptop where she was uploading pictures of her latest frames onto her website. It took her a minute to realize Matthew was back from guitar lessons already. The time had flown.

"Hi! How was your lesson?"

"Really good! Mrs. Singer said I totally aced the songs she assigned last week."

"Well done!"

"Thanks! Hey, she said that camp is filling up fast and we need to get my registration in as soon as possible or I might not get a spot."

"Oh, shoot, I totally forgot about that. Sorry. I'll try to look at it tonight. Can you remind me again before you go to bed?"

"I'll try. When's supper?"

Carrie's mind blanked. "Wow. I think I forgot about supper."

"It's your turn on the days I have lessons," he reminded her.

"Yeah, I guess I've got a lot going on right now…" she automatically tried to remember what her bank balance was. Old habits died hard. "So, can you live with pizza?"

"Sweet! Yeah! I'll just eat some bananas or something then. I want lots of room left for pizza." He left for the kitchen and was back in a minute with a banana in his hand and one in his mouth. "What's going on?"

"Hmmm?" Carrie answered absentmindedly. There. All the new items were posted and ready to be sold.

"You said you had a lot going on. What's up?"

Carrie sat back and looked at her son. How could he be so absent-minded about some things, and be so tuned in at other times? "Well, Jonathan and I are talking a lot about what's next for our family."

"Like more kids and stuff?"

She nodded. "These days there are lots of ways to grow a family. It's hard to think through and even harder to know what to do. Plus, anything we decide will have a big impact on you and Katie."

"How? I mean, is it just that you guys would have less time and money?"

Carrie did her best to explain some of their options and what it might mean for Matthew and his sister.

"I never thought about how lucky we are. We should share that with some other kids."

She put her arm around his waist and pulled him close. "You're awesome, you know that?"

"Yep. Do you need help ordering the pizza?"

"Ugh. I forgot already. No, I'll do it right now." She pulled out her phone and used their favorite pizza place's app to order pizza for delivery. Sometimes her new life felt worlds away from her old life.

The moment three years ago when she left a grocery store in tears because she had splurged on a cheap frozen pizza and blown the grocery budget would always be cemented in her mind.

It was one of her lowest points, when she felt like a failure as a mom and was constantly worried about money and whether she and the kids would survive. Desperate for even a few extra dollars she began pulling things out dumpsters, cleaning them up, and selling them.

That led to refinishing and selling furniture her friends and family donated without a second thought. Then, her miracle happened. She found a wad of cash in a second-hand side table that had been sitting in her parent's basement for years. While continuing to sell refinished furniture and expanding into creative picture frames to try to get out of debt, she used the money she found to finish her bachelor's degree and then her master's degree. Every single struggling step led her a little closer to providing for her kids and making things a little better.

Transformation. That's the word she and her friends had decided best described what they kept on doing. Transforming from one version of themselves to the next. Never losing who they were, but always finding something new and unexpected that they were capable of.

Carrie continued to think about everything as she set the table and waited for the delivery. At supper everyone was happy—they tried hard to make healthy meals at home, so pizza was a treat.

She watched Jonathan interact with the kids while they ate. He was such a natural as a dad. A part of her wanted to keep him just for Matthew and Katie. Matthew was right when he said that more kids would mean less time and money for them.

Pausing before taking another bite she shook her head. No, that wasn't true. They would still be able to pay for everything they needed—and most things they wanted. Although her work at the clinic paid a pittance, her private practice earned a good wage, and her business selling frames and artwork was thriving. Combine that with Jonathan's substantial earnings with his own internet security business, and finances weren't an issue for them at all.

"So, care to tell me what's filling your thoughts?" Jonathan asked as they settled into their loveseat at the end of the day. "You've been pretty quiet all evening."

"Well… I guess thinking about our future also has me thinking about my past. The last few years have been quite something."

"You can say that again." He leaned over and kissed her. "But that's because *you're* quite something. You know, we didn't talk that much about the other option for growing our family."

Carrie was confused. "What's that?"

"Fertility treatments and pregnancy. Well, maybe not treatments, but at least finding out if there's something with either of us that needs fixing."

"Oh."

"Is that an 'Oh we should do that'?"

"I… I don't think so. I mean, I'm pretty sure we couldn't start IVF until we've been trying for at least a year. And even if we did find something 'fixable', I don't think I'd want the expense or the physical and emotional cost of trying something that wasn't certain. That client of mine is who was doing IVF is separated from her husband now, and it may be because of the cost and stress of IVF treatments."

"That wouldn't be us, Carrie." He looked so devastated at the idea that Carrie regretted bringing it up. "But from what I understand, it's the woman who has to deal with the majority of the physical and emotional stuff. You do know we could fund a few treatments without it impacting our lifestyle though, right?"

Carrie nodded, even though she had a hard time believing it.

"But it really boils down to how important growing our family with pregnancies is to you."

"Actually, it's your say too. Right now you don't have any children that are genetically yours. Is that important to you?"

He chuckled. "Before I met you and the kids I would've said yes. But it's definitely not anymore. Matthew and Katie couldn't be more a part of me than they are now."

"Do you want to sit on this for a while and see if one of us changes our mind?"

"We can if you want to. But I'm OK to just take the next step now. Well, not now, but as soon as we figure out what the next step actually is!"

"I keep thinking about adopting from the state foster system," Carrie admitted. "I mean, we'd have to be super clear about what we could handle, and ready to say no if it's not right for our family. But, you know, it's like maybe our son our daughter is out there."

His smile lit up his entire face. "Really?"

"Yeah."

"That's what I kept going back to too. Carrie! Are we really going to do this?"

"Well, there's still no guarantee. We could be turned down —"

" —as if!"

She continued, "And we might not be matched with a child that's right for us."

"Oh. Right. But I want to try!"

"Me too, babe. Me too."

CHAPTER 10

Carrie woke up before her alarm, suddenly remembering her promise to Matthew about registering him for camp. She got up and made coffee and then came back to bed with two steaming mugs, the camp brochure, and her laptop.

"Hey," Jonathan mumbled, "I'm having an amazing dream that we're on our honeymoon and drinking coffee in bed. Don't wake me up."

She leaned over and kissed him. He smiled with his eyes still closed. Carrie took a moment to appreciate the view. His blond wavy hair was perfectly messy—he could get out of bed and go out in public and everyone would see him as the cool guy.

One muscular arm was outside the blanket. He still worked out a few times a week and claimed he wasn't half the guy he used to be, but Carrie thought he was in perfect shape. A blue eye opened.

"Mmmmm, in my dream a gorgeous woman is looking at me with very lusty eyes."

Carrie laughed loudly and then clamped her hand over her mouth. She wanted to enjoy this time with her husband without the kids joining them. "Shhhhh, you'll make me wake up the kids. Here, coffee."

He sat up and stretched before propping the pillows behind him and taking the coffee from Carrie. "Yep, this right here is luckiest man of the year material."

"Well, I did have an ulterior motive," she admitted.

He raised one eyebrow.

"Not that! We don't have enough time. I promised Matthew last night I'd do his band camp registration and then I forgot. At least if I do it now, I can tell him it's done when he wakes up."

She took a few sips of coffee, and then traded her mug for her laptop. Checking the brochure, she entered the camp's website. Immediately a slideshow of happy kids with instruments, quintessential summer activities, and professional-looking musicians began to play.

"Geez," Carrie whispered, "is this thing even real?"

"Looks like standard summer camp to me."

She looked at him, surprised. "Summer camp is really like that?"

"Of course! Why? Did you go to some camp from hell or something?"

"I never went to camp. It wasn't exactly an option in our family, especially for me. My summers were spend looking after Jessica."

Jonathan opened and closed his mouth a few times. "So, you're telling me you never went to summer camp."

"Correct. It wasn't that big a deal. We had really fun summers."

"Carrie, *everyone* has to go to summer camp. It's, like, a law or something."

"Well, call me a lawbreaker then. But seriously. This camp is $1,100.

Are you sure that's OK? We still want to put Katie in some camps. And go camping as a family."

"Check our bank balance," he answered with a resigned sigh.

Carrie opened a new tab and logged into their joint bank account. They had worked with Jenny to create a financial plan that suited both of them and their future goals. Carrie contributed 30% of the total family budget each month, and Jonathan contributed 70%. Their earnings above that were each spent individually.

Jonathan had insisted on Carrie knowing everything about his finances before they got married. He was proud of what he had accomplished, but more importantly he wanted Carrie to know she could trust him to always support the family financially.

As a single mom, Carrie had budgeted to the penny every month, often only having a few dollars to spare after paying all her expenses —on a good month. Now she was becoming so comfortable with their situation that she often forgot to check the bank balance for weeks at a time.

She was shocked to see $5,000 more in the account than she expected. "Jonathan! What's this?"

"It's the net sum of an invoice I was about to write off because I thought the client would never pay. Totally surprised me when it came in last week. I've been waiting for you to log in and be surprised ever since I deposited it!"

"Wow! Are you sure —"

"—Carrie, if you even think of questioning whether I should put all that in our joint account or not I will tickle you until you scream, and both kids will wake up before you get to register Matthew in camp."

Carrie mimed zipping her lips, but she couldn't keep the smile off her face. An extra $5,000? When did that ever happen to anybody? She confidently filled out the camp application and made an online payment for the full amount.

With a happy sigh she closed her laptop and picked up her coffee. "Bit of a change from when I was dreaming of having enough money to buy the kids beds so they wouldn't have to sleep on mattresses on the floor."

"You've come a long way baby."

"*We've* come a long way," she corrected him.

"Now let's talk about where you're going for summer camp."

"There's no such thing as summer camp for moms!"

"Then start one! I know for sure Lisa's never been to summer camp —not with the dad she had. Kara and Jenny probably have, but they deserve a break anyways. Maybe Jaz went to some strict extra tutoring camp or something, but I'll bet she never went to a camp just for fun. And Lauren definitely needs a break. Come on. The last time you ladies put your minds to something you bought a vacant building and turned it into affordable housing for six families. I'm pretty sure you could plan a moms' summer camp if you tried."

Carrie drank her cooling coffee and tried to think of how she could disagree with Jonathan. Summer camp for moms? That sounded selfish. But then he'd remind her about all the years she didn't treat herself at all. It also sounded expensive. But knowing their bank balance right now she couldn't use that argument.

"For it to truly be a break, Lisa couldn't come with Marcus and Jaz couldn't come with Alex. It's just not fair to invite them knowing they don't have childcare. And I wouldn't plan anything and *not* invite them." There. That should take care of things.

"Oh. Couldn't Jaz leave Alex with her parents?"

"I don't think she'd want to with her dad travelling to wherever their factory is. And her mom still works full-time."

"And I don't think I could take Marcus. I'm happy to be on baby duty with you around, but without you? No way. But I'll bet Max would take him! He'd have to take time off to stay with Angela anyways."

"Wouldn't you take Angela here? You're the one with the flexible schedule. And Max will want to bank any days off for when their baby comes."

"Ah. Right. I was going to say that I could take Alex. He loves Matthew and Katie and doesn't hate me, so he'd be happy here."

"You're still forgetting two people. Dustin and Brittany. Lauren's Dustin's primary caregiver. And even though Dustin can do a lot of things for Brittany, I don't think he could go solo for days. Even if he didn't need help with his own personal care."

"Oh yeah. Shoot. OK. Let me think about this. There's got to be a solution."

"Why are you so crazy about this? I get breaks all the time now when you take the kids out so I can work, and when we go out as a family. Shoot, just having someone make meals and share housework is like a holiday for me!"

He pointed his finger at her. "That's why. Because you think that shared housework is a break, not a right." He put his empty coffee mug down on the night table and turned to face her. "And because sometimes when I think about the crap you went through with Don it makes me feel really helpless because I can't go back in time and take that out of your life. So, if there's something good I can do for you now, I'm going to do it."

She snuggled into him. "I'm the luckiest woman in the world for sure."

"I thought you said we didn't have time to..."

Carrie caught his teasing glance before he could hide it. "You're right, we don't! You make sure the kids are up. I'm going to pop in the shower."

They slipped into their daily routine and Carrie forgot about Mom Camp.

"I've got it!" Jonathan shouted as he ran up the stairs from his office where he had been working all morning.

Carrie was in the kitchen baking chocolate chip cookies in advance of Matthew having a few friends over after school.

"Got what?"

"I've got the camp solution all figured out!" he announced proudly while grabbing two cookies from the cooling rack.

"OK …." Carrie turned to look at him.

He held one finger up to pause her and closed his eyes as he slowly ate the cookies. When we was finished he opened his eyes, "OK, I'm all for equality, but there's no way I can bake as good as you. Please, please, please bake for me forever."

"You are turning out to be far easier to please than I expected!" she joked. "Now, what's this camp thing?"

"The childcare! It took a few phone calls, but we figured it out! Hang on, I made notes," he pulled his phone out of his back pocket. "First of all, your parents are coming for the whole time. Then, Max is going to make sure he's only working locally. He'll take Marcus for the nights, and we'll watch Marcus and Angela here with your mom's help when he's working."

Carrie opened her mouth, but he put a finger over her lips and kept talking.

"During the day your dad's going to be at Lauren and Dustin's. He'll help them out, and bring Brittany here for nighttime. Oh, we're going to have Alex here, and if her parents want to help out at all they are welcome to. Jaz's mom is at work right now so I couldn't confirm anything with her. Ken's pretty much got his hands full because the older boys have rugby and he's coaching, but he's available for anything else we might need when he's not coaching."

He put the phone down, clearly pleased with all he had accomplished.

Carrie went around the island and sat on a stool. "Wow. That's … that's a lot of kids coming in and out of here. My mom is going to be in her glory!"

"Oh yeah, and if Maria doesn't want to go to camp with you all, she can hang out here too. Might as well make use of the fact that this house is wheelchair accessible."

"And everyone's on board with this idea of sending their partners to camp for a few days?"

"More than OK. They thought it was a great idea! We all agreed you need to be away for at least four full days to make it worthwhile. That doesn't include travel time."

"I swear I've been abducted by aliens and put on a different planet. This is not normal husband behavior. You realize that, right?"

"You're wrong. All the other stuff is not normal husband behavior. *We're* the right ones. It's just that there's not that many of us—yet. So, call the girls, get together, and book wherever you're going. We need some time to make sure we coordinate our work schedules."

Carrie felt sure they guys were missing something but she couldn't think of what it was. "Uh, can you send that plan to me? I had a little trouble keeping track of it all."

"Of course. Max made a 24-hour spreadsheet with all the kids and adults and where everyone is. It's pretty easy to follow."

Jonathan practically danced back down the stairs, but Carrie stayed fixed to her chair until the timer went for the cookies. She took them out of the oven, put another tray in, set the timer, and then slowly moved the cookies onto cooling racks. There didn't seem to be any choice but to get together with her friends and see what they thought.

CHAPTER 11

"Wow," Carrie said to herself as she pulled into Lisa's driveway. "I swear she's doubled the flowers in the front yard since last year."

She got out and took a few minutes to enjoy the vibrant front yard before knocking on the door.

Maria opened it and wheeled her chair back so Carrie could come in. "Hi Maria," she said, leaning down for a hug. "You're looking gorgeous!" She could hear happy baby squeals from the upstairs bathroom.

"Thank you! Jaz had me in her studio today modeling the new fall clothes for her accessible line. There was a professional hair stylist, and another person who did my makeup. I thought it was perfect timing with you all coming over tonight so I could show it off!"

"Well, she couldn't have chosen a better model. You're going to have the line sold out in no time!"

"Oh you," Maria answered, brushing her away with her hand. But Carrie could see how pleased she was with the compliment.

"Hey, I was hoping someone would come early and take baby duty."

Carrie looked up to see Lisa at the top floor landing, holding baby Marcus bundled up in a towel. "I'm on my way," she said, quickly slipping off her flats and dropping her purse. She ran upstairs and went into the nursery where Lisa was dressing Marcus.

"Thanks! Here, can you take him downstairs and I'll come down in a minute? I need to put a dry shirt on. Haven't quite figured out how to *not* give myself a bath at the same time as him."

Carrie watched as Lisa deftly dressed a very wiggly Marcus and then gladly took him in her arms. He looked at her with big brown eyes, aware that this wasn't one of the faces he knew. "Just wait until he can really splash. Then you'll need a blow dryer along with a change of clothes."

"I can't wait!" Lisa said over her shoulder as she walked into her room. Carrie believed her.

Soon the rest of the ladies were all taking turns holding the baby, and Carrie was glad she had come early enough to have a bit of time with him without having to share. Maria pulled her wheelchair beside where Carrie was sitting at the end of the loveseat.

"So, how's the adjustment to married life going?" she asked.

"You mean, has reality finally set in that I don't have to do it all myself anymore?"

Maria nodded, smiling.

"Honestly Maria, it still feels like a dream most days. I just … I knew my first marriage was dysfunctional, but it seems like every day Jonathan shows me another way that a good marriage is supposed to work that I haven't even thought of. He insists that we share everything equally. Meals, childcare, driving, cleaning."

"I'd find that quite strange, too. Is there any sort of de-programming women can have after being in bad relationships so they can see a good relationship as normal and not exceptional or unusual?"

"If there isn't, there should be," Carrie agreed. "It's a case of really not knowing how much I didn't know."

"Well, I'm so happy you get to experience it all now."

Lauren sat down on the chair beside Maria and asked her about a new physiotherapy clinic she had started attending and Carrie sat back, thinking. It seemed like she did more thinking now than she ever had before.

Maria had been trapped in a controlling, abusive marriage for over twenty years. Her husband had even threatened to take Lisa away when he saw how much Maria doted on her young daughter. She had withdrawn from Lisa and lived in constant fear of losing her. The day of her high school graduation, Lisa ran away, believing that neither of her parents loved her.

When Lisa's dad suddenly died, she reluctantly came home for the funeral and found her mom in desperate need of care and companionship. She adjusted her own life goals, took her mother in, and the two of them began a journey of healing and transformation. Carrie knew that Maria and Lisa never took their new relationship for granted after all the years they had lost.

Her thoughts were interrupted when Jaz came in. "Hi everyone! Sorry I'm late." She made a striking grand entrance without even trying. With her signature bob, micro bangs, and custom-designed wardrobe in her favorite black and white palette, she always looked ready to jump on a fashion runway.

They all greeted her, and she went into the kitchen for a minute before coming out with a coffee. She sat down beside Carrie.

"Hey, it's been forever since I've seen you!"

"I know! Not since we all went out for dessert together on Valentine's day!"

Jaz rolled her eyes. "I still can't believe you spent your first Valentine's as a married women out with your friends instead of your husband."

"Well, we did have all day when the kids were at school to celebrate." Carrie gave Jaz a meaningful look.

"Aw, that's so… Oh. OH!"

Carrie laughed as she saw a blush glow beneath Jaz's dark skin. "And it's all your fault for making me go on that first date with Jonathan."

"OK, gross stuff aside, I will definitely take all the credit for that. You look great by the way."

"Thanks, so do you, as usual."

"Hey Carrie," Lauren called out, "did you have something to talk about, or were we just overdue for girls' time."

"Both actually. There's no rush for my stuff, though."

Jenny walked in from the kitchen with a tray of baked goods from Maria's favorite bakery. In her other hand was a stack of delicate napkins with blue and white flowers. "I think we should get right to it after everyone's helped themselves. If it's anything like the housing project, we'll need lots of time to talk about it."

After everyone had something to eat, Carrie started. "So, this is an absolute crazy idea, but Jonathan thinks we should all go away to summer camp together."

There was total silence as everyone looked at her.

"It all started when he found out I never went to summer camp as a kid. He said it was a requirement for life and I had to go. Now. As a grown-up. And he thought all of you should go too. I told him it wouldn't work because we're all responsible for taking care of other people."

"True. I don't make any plans for Ken and I to go away unless I've got my help lined up from all of you," Kara said.

"Yeah. Well, apparently he saw that as a challenge. So he's been calling all of your people and they think they've got it figured out."

She took out her phone and read out the schedule the guys had prepared. "Well, that's it. That's my big announcement. Can you think of anything more crazy?"

"I'm in!" Lauren blurted out.

"What?"

"I've been going nuts. If I'm at home, someone needs me. If I'm out, I'm stressing about someone needing me. You could stick me in a tent in the woods with a shovel and a roll of toilet paper for a week and I'd be happy."

"Whoa now," Jenny said. "There's no way I'm doing tenting and no running water. Lauren, you've got more guts than I'll ever have."

"Water," Lisa offered. "It needs to be near water. Like a gentle river, or a lake or something."

"Can we have someone cook for us?" Kara asked. "I'd love to have a few days where I didn't have to cook or wash dishes."

"Wait a minute," Carrie piped up. "You guys are actually considering this?"

"Duh." Lauren answered.

Soon everyone was talking at once, giving ideas and all sorts of reasons why they were desperate for a break.

Jaz leaned closer to Carrie, "You didn't mean me too, did you?"

"Of course! It wouldn't be the same without you, and Jonathan's already got Alex's care figured out." She looked at Jaz carefully. "But no work allowed. Not even a single email."

Jaz's eyes got wide.

"Carrie!" Jenny called from across the room. "Is there a date for camp?"

"No, but the guys need one as soon as possible so they can book their work schedules and stuff."

"I'm afraid I only have one week in July that will work," Kara said.

Everyone spoke at once, but the consensus seemed to be that July was perfect.

"I've got a few things to say," Maria started. "First off, I won't come." Lauren started to protest. "No, no, you can't change my mind. I need my own bed every night, and I find travel really hard on my body. But I think of all of you I have the most time free to plan this camp, and that would make me really feel like I'm still a part of it."

Carrie leaned over and hugged Maria. "You'll be very missed if you're not there. I hadn't said anything because I wanted you to come, but Jonathan suggested you spend the days at our place. An extra body around will be really helpful with all the kids, and you can visit with my mom."

Maria smiled. "That sounds wonderful! It would be rather quiet here with everyone gone. I'll book the accessible taxi early so I can come and go on my own." She looked around the room. "Well then, I'm going to need a bit of information from everyone. What your budget is, what type of accommodations you want, any special food needs, activities you'd most like to do—"

"—Sleep!" Lisa said with a laugh. "All I want is sleep. Oh, and coffee, and all of you!"

"It's true, having Marcus does interrupt our sleep cycles. OK, I'll make sure the place has good reviews about their beds. I think if everyone could email their list to me that would be best. Oh, this is so exciting!"

CHAPTER 12

"So, everyone's on board with camp?" Jonathan asked that night.

"Totally. Maria won't go because it's too hard on her to travel and sleep in a bed that isn't her own, but she offered to take care of all the planning. Knowing her, the planning will make her over-the-moon happy. And she loves the idea of coming over here during the day. She's probably already booked the accessible taxi."

"I can always borrow your parent's van and drive her."

"That's a good back-up. But I think she wants to be in control of when she comes and goes. She looks really good, but I noticed her mobility is definitely deteriorating. So wherever she can have some control will be good for her."

"Fair enough."

She paused. "In other news, I was thinking about having a family ice cream sundae party sometime this weekend so we can talk to the kids about adopting."

Jonathan laughed. "I thought you were going to say so we could talk to the kids about you going to camp and was wondering if you were making a bit too big of a deal over it!"

"Oh, it's definitely a big deal, but I don't think the kids are going to have any issues with it. In fact, they're probably going to count the days until I leave. Although, yeah, we could talk about it. You really did set yourself up when you watched them when I went to help look after Mom last year before our wedding. They're going to expect that level of fun every time I go away!"

"Much better than having them chase your car down the road calling for you to come back!"

"Very true. But back to the adoption thing. I keep struggling with giving them enough information to be prepared but not so much that they are terrified."

"Hmmm, you've got a point. At least we can count on Katie to launch random questions by the dozen, so we'll have a chance to figure everything out that we haven't figured out yet ..."

"And Matthew?"

"Yeah. Matthew's a different story. You may need to plan a few mom dates with him in the next few weeks so he can talk things out. He'll need time to process everything."

"Fortunately these things move pretty slowly so we'll all have time to process things."

"And in the meantime you have camp to look forward to!"

Carrie smiled. "Yes. In the meantime I have camp."

The next day Jonathan took Katie to gymnastics and came home with a bag of sundae making supplies.

"Mommy! Matthew!" Katie shouted as soon as she walked in the door, "Daddy bought lots and lots of treats and we're having an ice cream party!"

"Go wash your hands and change out of your leotard while I set things up, OK?" Jonathan asked.

"OK! Matthew! Ice cream!"

"I'm coming!" he said, jogging down the stairs. He joined Carrie and Jonathan in the dining room. "Why the family meeting?"

"It's *not* a family meeting!" Carrie insisted. "It's a family ice cream party!"

His eyes narrowed, "So you don't have any big news to talk about? No family decisions to make?"

"Well ..." she stalled.

"Yep. Family meeting. Called it." He held up his hand for a high five and Carrie reluctantly returned it.

"Yeah yeah. Smarty pants."

"I got mini M&M's," Jonathan quipped. "Sorry, no Smarties."

A few minutes later Carrie drizzled chocolate syrup over the ribbons of caramel syrup that were sitting on top of a scoop of vanilla and a scoop of chocolate ice cream. Beside her Katie was happily sprinkling mini M&M's on top of the rainbow sprinkles and mini marshmallows that were nearly hiding her ice cream.

"We should have ice cream sundaes every Saturday!" she exclaimed.

"Totally," Matthew agreed. "Except the other ones should be *just* ice cream sundae days." He gave Carrie a meaningful look.

"So ..." Carrie began in between spoonfuls, "this summer me and all the other moms I'm friends with are going to camp together!"

Katie giggled. "Mommy Camp?"

"Kind of. We're all going to go away for a few days and do fun stuff together."

"Can I go to Mommy Camp when I'm grown up?"

"Of course!" *Wow,* she thought, *One decision and suddenly I'm changing my daughter's future too.*

"Who'll watch everyone else's kids?" Matthew asked. "I mean, we're good with Jonathan, but what about Lisa and Jaz? Are they going?"

"Of course they're going! All the dads got together and figured out a whole schedule. Your dad can show it to you if you want. You guys will have the most fun, though. Grandma and Grandpa are coming to help out, Alex is going to sleep over here, and Brittany, Marcus, and Angela will be here during the daytime."

Matthew looked at Jonathan. "Are you crazy?"

"Probably."

Katie held up her fingers. "That's … um … that's two more grown-ups and four more kids! That's a big playdate!"

"Yep. One big happy playdate." Jonathan agreed.

"Is that all?" Matthew asked as he added more ice cream and M&M's to his bowl.

"No. Your mom and I have been talking a lot about growing our family, and we've decided to start the application process to adopt!"

"Mommy's tummy isn't going to grow a baby?"

Carrie's eyes grew wide as she realized she needed to get on birth control right away. She definitely didn't want to run the risk of adopting *and* having a baby at the same time. One look at Jonathan and she knew he was thinking the same thing.

"Probably not. It's not a no forever on having a baby from my tummy. But there are kids already living in our city who are waiting for a family. We think maybe one of those kids is meant for us!"

"Will they call you Daddy and Mommy and I'll be their sister and Matthew will be their brother?"

"That depends. They might be older, and still have memories of their first Mommy and Daddy. We'd call them their birth Mommy and birth Daddy because they were born from them. So they might feel better calling us Carrie and Jonathan. But we'd still be their family. It just might take a while for them to feel like they're family. We'd have to be patient."

Katie sighed. "I'm very unpatient."

"Impatient," Carrie corrected.

"How long does it take?" Matthew asked.

"Quite a while. Your mom and I will have a lot of paperwork to fill out. Then there's interviews, and the adoption worker will want to talk to you two, and make sure our house is safe for another child. So, it's May right now. Probably not until next year is my guess."

"That's a long time." Katie's mouth drooped for a second. "Where would they sleep? In my room?"

"We were thinking that Matthew could move into the guest room and they'd have Matthew's room."

"But then Grandma and Grandpa can't visit!"

"Sure they can. When they visit, Matthew can sleep on the floor in your room, or in the basement." Jonathan turned to Matthew. "And at some point we can build you a room in that big open area in the basement. There will come a time when you'll want a bit of space between you and your younger siblings."

"Cool." Matthew nodded his agreement. He reached for the ice cream scoop.

"I think two bowls is enough, bud," Carrie said.

He reluctantly took his hand back and proceeded to carefully scoop every last drop from his bowl. Katie picked her bowl up and licked it before Carrie could stop her.

"Now you've got ice cream from your forehead to your chin!"

Katie grinned in response.

"OK, everyone help clean up and go get your Saturday chores done."

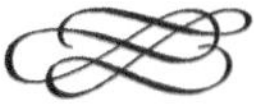

CHAPTER 13

Carrie and Jonathan were required to attend an adoption information session before they could begin the application process, so they decided to combine it with date night. After leaving the meeting they went to their favorite fusion restaurant for a late dinner.

They each ordered a drink, and then both started talking at once.

"You start," Jonathan insisted.

"OK. I just have to say that I don't ever want to be that woman. The one who seemed like she lived and breathed children and couldn't talk beyond that."

"What, nine kids isn't your idea of a good time?" he teased. "But I totally agree. That wouldn't be fair to Matthew and Katie, and I'm not willing to share you that much. No matter what, we need to make sure we always have time together."

Carrie nodded. "And I think you either have to be ridiculously organized to do what she does, or ridiculously laid back. Both traits I do not have. The other couples, I felt like I could relate to better. It helped to hear about the hard times, and not just have them paint this rosy picture that isn't believable."

"Yeah, I was hoping to ask the guy who adopted after they had three by birth what it was like, but he was kind of mobbed by people so I didn't get the chance."

"Which is kind of how we got stuck looking at the album." Carrie slowly turned her glass of wine. "I knew that would suck."

"Yeah. I kept remembering what Mark said about baby selling."

"Well, giving potential adoptive parents a massive album full of pictures of adorable kids just waiting for their forever family is a pretty good technique."

"I tried to not look too closely, but that was impossible. And then the woman beside me was like, 'oh there aren't very many with blond hair' and I had to walk away," Jonathan said.

"Wow. Hey, how do you feel about the whole 'kids who don't look like us' thing?"

He looked at the art on the wall beside him for a moment before answering. "For me personally it really doesn't matter. Kids are kids. They need homes, they need love. What they look like doesn't change that."

"But …" Carrie prompted.

"But what if *they* care? What if they really want parents who look like them? What if being in a family where you look totally different from your parents and siblings creates problems? I'd feel terrible forcing a kid into a situation like that."

"Some people are always going to be asses," Carrie agreed. "But skin color seems to bring out a special kind of ass. I mean, Jaz has to deal with racist comments. She has her whole life."

Jonathan's eyebrows went up. "Really?"

Carrie nodded.

"So what do you think?" he asked.

"About appearances? I'm like you, only without the 'but'. We do what's right for us and our children—even if one of those children comes from another tummy, as Katie would say. You can get harassed for all kinds of things these days. If it's because one of our kids looks different then we'll deal with it. I hate to even think about it, but some kids are going to have things harder because of the way they look. At least if they're with someone like us, they won't have to face it alone."

"Have I ever told you what an amazing woman you are?"

"Yes. But I never get tired of hearing it."

He leaned over and kissed her cheek. "You, Carrie Brandt are an amazing woman. And an amazing wife. And an amazing mother. Whoever we adopt will have hit the lottery with you."

"So, how tempted will you be to start the adoption application paperwork tonight?" she teased.

"Well … I mean … I thought I'd look over it." he said sheepishly, as the server brought their entrees. They both started eating before he continued. "To be honest, I always struggled with answering those types of questions. You know, stuff like 'why should you be allowed to adopt' and 'what are you most likely to screw up on as a dad'. I think you have a huge advantage over me because you answered questions like that all the time for your degree. Give me a technical question any day over all of this personal stuff."

"Huh," Carrie replied, "I did *not* know that about you. I'd offer to help you with your portion of the application, but I think they'd be able to tell it was me."

"Plus, that would be the adoption application equivalent of cheating," he said, jokingly giving her a disapproving look.

She pointed her fork at him, "You have a point. Sorry. You're all on your own with that pile of paperwork."

When they got home, Matthew was sitting on the floor leaning against the couch, watching TV with Maisy curled up beside him.

Carrie and Jonathan had almost given in on the 'no dogs on the couch' rule, but decided that the furniture needed to be a safe place for any child they might adopt if they were afraid of dogs. So cuddles with Maisy were limited to on the floor.

"Hey you," Carrie said, walking in and kissing him on the forehead. "How was everything?"

"Good! Katie tried to tell me there was a new rule that she got two bowls of ice cream but I wouldn't let her."

"Good for you. I'm going to make a cup of tea and go to bed. Thanks for watching Katie and Maisy."

"No problem."

Jonathan came and sat on the couch beside Matthew. "What are you watching?"

"*Spiderman Far From Home.*"

"Cool. I haven't seen that one." He leaned back and turned towards the kitchen. "Carrie —"

"Go ahead!" she answered with a smile. Although she had no problem sitting and watching superhero movies with Matthew, she was happy to skip this one. Instead, she'd drink her tea and flip through a home decorating magazine that had been sitting on her nightstand unopened for almost a week.

After a quick check on Katie — who had thrown off her blankets and was sprawled across her bed — Carrie got ready for bed and settled in for some quiet time. But her mind wouldn't stop wandering to the pictures in that album, and the stories from other adoptive parents.

The idea that there were children in the same city as her, right now, who had gone to bed without a mom or dad to tuck them in was almost unbearable. Like the meeting facilitator had said, 'even children in good foster homes know they are temporary family members'.

How do those children even go to school every day without getting an 'I love you' from their parents? What happens when they get sick? Is there anyone who stops everything to rub their back when their tummy hurts? And what about special occasions? Are they celebrated? Do they have anything to look forward to?

It was all overwhelming. Maybe that was the point. She knew the foster system was overwhelmed. Shoot, even Mark, operating a private foster agency where he *could* say no to cases, never said no. She couldn't blame him.

Then she remembered what he said about Bethany and Marcus, 'Marcus already has a better chance at life than his mom or grandma'. That, she could handle. With Jonathan, the kids, and their friends and family, they could give one child a better chance at life. Whatever happened, at least she would know that.

CHAPTER 14

"Carrie?" Jonathan called from the dining room table where he had been sitting for the past two hours filling out forms.

"Hey there," she said, walking into the room. "Katie's asleep already. I think she's coming down with something."

"Did you check her temperature?"

"Yep, all normal. She's just tired and not her usual bouncy self."

"Poor thing."

"What did you want?"

"Have you gotten to the part in the adoption application about what you want in a child?" he asked.

"No. What does it ask, like age and gender and stuff?"

"If the stuff includes every possible trait and history of the child, then yes. This is brutal Carrie. It's like a shopping list but for a real living, breathing child."

Carrie sat down beside him and looked over the questions. "Well…

let's start with the questions we can easily answer and go from there. I'll go get my application. I need to finish it soon anyways."

When she came back there were two glasses of wine waiting. "Not that this drives me to drink or anything," Jonathan said sheepishly, "but I thought it might help lift the mood."

"I'm not complaining. OK, age of the child. I think it works best if it's someone younger than Katie."

"Agreed. So we can put zero to seven."

"Gender—either one, right?"

Jonathan nodded. "Now this is where it gets tricky. Prenatal exposure to alcohol and drugs. I know you said you were fine with drug exposure but aren't we saying no to a lot of kids if we say no to alcohol exposure?"

Carrie put her hand on Jonathan's arm. "Hon, we're may say no to a lot of kids regardless. I think we need to try to be logical about this, not emotional. We have to think about what will work for us and the kids."

"You're right. OK, drug exposure is a yes, alcohol is a no. What's next … Tobacco exposure? Really? Am I stereotyping if I say most kids in the system have birth parents who smoked?"

"I don't know the statistics, but it seems possible. I think tobacco exposure is OK."

"Oh boy. The next section asks about conception by incest. I'm starting to feel like I've lived the first 34 years of my life in a very naïve bubble."

"I *think* that one's fine. Let's see … Oh, now we get to shop for appearance. Geez. Well, I say we don't put any limitations here. Besides, we've already talked about this. OK, next is disabilities. What do you think?"

"You have experience as a caregiver already with your mom. And our house is wheelchair accessible. And we have pretty flexible work schedules. The physical disabilities I think we can manage. But the other things?"

Carrie tried to remain neutral and not let her emotions mess with her thoughts. "I don't think we can do autism. Aaron's such an amazing Dad to Thea, but I couldn't do what he does. I think I'm the same for the rest of these." She wrapped her arms around her waist for a few seconds before Jonathan nodded and they both marked more boxes as 'no'. Her stomach was a bit achy. "I feel like I've just said 'nope, you don't get to come home with me' to kids over and over again."

Jonathan looked at her sympathetically. "Remember, it's about what's right for us, too. And I think this *is* the right choice for us. Doesn't make it easy or comfortable, thought." He reached over and caressed her cheek before looking back at the forms. "The last one is sibling groups. I hadn't even thought about more than one."

"I think we'd better say no to more than one. This will be a huge change for all of us—including the child. I want to be able to do it right."

"One it is. Alright. That's truly all I can handle tonight." He stood up and stacked everything carefully. "I'd think we should keep this in our office now that I know what the questions are. We don't need to stress out the kids with all of this by leaving it lying around."

"Good point. I'll take our glasses and meet you upstairs."

It took almost two more weeks to get everything completed.

"OK, I think this is it." Jonathan set a stack of papers nearly an inch tall on the table. "This is worse than university papers!"

"Maybe they weed out uncommitted potential parents this way," Carrie suggested.

He snorted. "Might actually work."

She took the top piece of paper. "Alright, let's check things off one at a time. My personal application."

"Check."

"My criminal record check, then my medical reference, then my personal references."

"Hang on. You're already going too fast. OK… check, check, and check."

They repeated the process with Jonathan's portion of the application, and then moved to the next section. This included copies of their bank statements, a credit report, an application with joint questions, and two sheets of questions that Matthew had to fill out.

"Well, all we have to do now is take the online classes, pass the homestudy and personal interviews, and get in line for our next child!"

"At least I'm used to online learning!" Carrie joked. She had taken her bachelor's degree and master's degree online, and loved the chance to study on her own time without having to leave the house and her kids.

"I'd like to do it at the same time, if that's OK?" Jonathan asked.

"Oh, I hadn't thought of that. Why?"

"Well, you know how long it took me to fill out the application? I think it might take me a while to get through the classes, and maybe if you're there to talk me through it I won't hold up the process so much."

"Jonathan, you are not holding up the process. I'm certain that when this is all said and done the timing's going to work out perfectly. Hey, the right child for us might not even be legally available for adoption yet. Don't feel pressured. I'll definitely help you out, but whenever this happens, it happens."

"When did you get so smart?"

She smiled at him. "Baby, I've *always* been smart. I'm just even smarter now than I used to be."

CHAPTER 15

"They're here! They're here!" Katie shouted from her bedroom window where she had been watching the driveway for the last half hour. She came tearing down the stairs and nearly had a collision with Maisy, who was jumping up and down, just as excited.

Jonathan was first to the door. "OK, Katie. Are you ready for this?"

Katie nodded, suddenly completely serious.

"What's the first thing to do?"

"Get a treat!" she shouted, and then tried again. "Get a treat," she said in a quieter voice. She went to the tin by the door and took a dog treat out. Immediately she had Maisy's undivided attention.

"Maisy sit." she commanded and Maisy dropped her backside. Her tailed continued to wag furiously. Katie broke off a piece of the treat and gave it to Maisy. "Maisy heel." she said and then put the treat in her fist and dropped it to her side. Immediately Maisy was standing at her side. Slowly Katie opened the door and walked outside. Maisy followed in a perfect heel.

"Hi Grandpa and Grandma," Katie called in a restrained voice, "I have to be calm so Maisy knows I'm in charge. I'm coming to say hi." She walked carefully around to the side of the van where her Grandma was just being lowered in her wheelchair.

Jonathan, Carrie, and Matthew all followed quietly behind. Jonathan had grabbed a few back-up treats. Carrie and Matthew were both holding their breath. Controlling Maisy was an essential part of her training, but they still felt unsure outside of their fenced backyard or the dog training facility.

"Maisy, this is Grandma. Sit." But Maisy didn't seem happy about the wheelchair. She backed up a few steps and then turned to the side with a whine. "Maisy, sit!" Katie tried with a firmer voice.

Jonathan was just about to step in and pick up Maisy when Katie figured out what was going on. She crouched beside the dog and started stroking her head. "That's a wheelchair. It's Grandma's legs, and she needs it. Just because you never seen one before doesn't mean it's bad." Maisy reached up and gave Katie's cheek a lick. "OK Maisy, I have a treat for you but you have to sit first, OK?" The puppy looked in Katie's eyes for a second before slowly sitting down. Katie rewarded her with her treat and then Jonathan picked up Maisy before she decided to go for a run.

"That was the most impressive feat of dog training I've ever seen!" Grandpa was the first to speak. "Are you free to give me a hug now?"

"Yes Grandpa, but I have to not yell because I think Maisy's still a little scared."

They all hugged and made their way into the house. Carrie glowed with pride as her mom easily navigated up the permanent ramp along the side of the house to the front door, and then into the house. One of Jonathan's biggest gifts to her before they got married was re-doing parts of his newly renovated home so that Carrie's parents could visit whenever they wanted.

Even though they only lived an hour away, they had never seen their grandchildren's home until the past year. Now, with a completely level first floor including an accessible powder room, and a stair lift that took her mom upstairs to a fully accessible guest suite with its own bathroom, Carrie's parents could come over whenever they wanted.

There was just time for lunch together before Jaz and Lisa arrived and the three of them left for Mom camp. They settled at the table while Carrie tossed the chicken Caesar salad she had prepared for lunch. For the second time in a year she'd have several days in a row without any responsibilities or meals to prepare. The last one had been her honeymoon in November. Part of her felt like she really didn't deserve it. Her life was so good already! But then, maybe that's what made a good life even better—more good things.

"So," Carrie's mom began as soon as they were served, "have you heard anything about your adoption application?"

Jonathan answered, "Nothing. Carrie even called the department last week to double check that they had all our paperwork and didn't need anything else."

"We know they're overworked," Carrie added, "but you'd think that approving adoptive parents and helping children leave the system for permanent homes would be a priority."

"Maybe they're too busy putting out fires," her dad suggested.

"Why are there fires?" Katie asked, suddenly worried. "Is my sister-brother going to get hurt?" After many discussions about what type of child might join their family, she coined the term sister-brother to describe them so she wouldn't leave anyone out.

"Grandpa means urgent things that come up that need to be dealt with right away. Not actual fires," Jonathan explained.

"Well, we're so proud of you all for thinking about growing your family this way, and we can't wait to see our new grandchild—whenever they arrive," Carrie's mom said. "And now we get five whole days together with our favorite grandchildren. And some extras to boot! How fun!"

"You guys are going to be raising the roof here while I sit in a chair on the beach with the girls. I'm not sure how the universe flipped on its side to make that happen. Actually it was all Jonathan's idea, so no matter how things turn out he gets all the credit!"

They had just finished cleaning up lunch when the doorbell rang. Katie was there in a flash. "My grammy and grandpa are already here so we can have the babies now!"

"Is Alex still a baby?" Jaz asked as she set down the two-year-old and tried to hold him still while she took off his sandals. As soon as she let him go, he took off after Maisy, arms stretched straight out.

Katie was torn, unsure whether to go after Alex or wait for Lisa to take Marcus out of his infant car seat.

"I don't think he knows what to do with a puppy," Jaz warned.

Katie ran after him, decision made. In her place everyone else crowded into the entry way.

"I'll unload the gear," Jonathan offered, and Carrie's dad was quick to follow.

"Good thing you're here, Mom," Carrie said with a smile. "I think they both just realized what they got themselves into!"

"I've been looking forward to this since Jonathan called me!" she answered. "Here Lisa, if I can hold Marcus you'll have both hands free."

Lisa unbuckled him and handed him over. He lay there, looking intensely at the new face. "I'll bet you're going to be his favorite, especially if you can get Katie to push you around. Wheels are definitely his thing!"

The men appeared at the door with armloads of gear, and everyone got busy planning where things should go and setting things up.

"It's a good thing Max and Jenny have already got all the gear for their baby!" Lisa exclaimed, "I don't think I could've packed one more thing in the car!"

"These men who are so capable," Carrie's mom marveled. "I thought it was a big deal when John asked me to show him how to change a diaper. It would never have occurred to us to leave him home alone with a baby for a week, let alone a baby and a toddler."

"Well, Angela's eight, so I think she'll be a huge help to Max."

"Speaking of leaving, I'm going to go grab my stuff." Carrie jogged up the stairs. Seeing Alex's things already set up in their master bedroom made her pause for a moment. She would love to be here with Jonathan and see how they worked together when more kids were in the picture. Maybe it was an *if* more kids came at this point. Whenever their application was approved, they still had their online courses and then the homestudy, and then maybe another long wait to find out if they were approved. "Better enjoy the life we have now," she reminded herself as she grabbed the suitcase that was packed and waiting.

"Here," Jonathan said, reaching for her suitcase. He took it from her and went to load it in Lisa's car.

Carrie had been bracing for a tearful goodbye from Katie. Instead, she had to grab her for a quick kiss and a hug in between Katie chasing Alex and gazing at Marcus. Matthew was the one who seemed more reluctant for Carrie to leave.

"It's going to be quite a different week for you," Carrie said quietly.

He nodded. "Will it always be this loud?"

"Well, Angela will be here during the daytime, oh, Maria will prob-ably be over too. They're both quiet, but more people is still more people. But remember, your room is your safe zone. Whenever you're feeling overwhelmed it's totally OK for you to take a break. Put on your headphones, play some guitar, and only join the crowd when you're ready, OK?"

"OK Mom. I love you. Have a good time at camp." The corner of his mouth twitched. He'd been teasing Carrie about being too old for camp since she first told him about it.

"Thanks bud. I'll probably just sleep and sit in a rocker all week since I'm so old…"

He smiled and gave her a tight hug. Minutes later Carrie was in the passenger seat of Lisa's car as they pulled away from the house.

"Wow," Lisa breathed. "I wasn't prepared for feeling … I think I'm feeling sad about going! I haven't left Marcus alone ever, and now I'm leaving him for five nights and four days all at once!"

"I've been counting the days since May," Jaz said from the backseat. "It was definitely easier for me when Alex was a baby because I had you and your mom to watch him whenever I needed."

"And now you have a good daycare *and* babysitters!" Lisa said. "I'm going to have to take lessons from you on that."

"Even with all of that I'm still having a hard time keeping up with everything," Jaz admitted.

Carrie turned to reassure her. "Jaz! That couldn't possibly be your laptop!"

"Sorry. I know we said no work, but I've got some emails I have to deal with and then I'll shut it down and leave it in Lisa's trunk. I'll be done before we get there."

"I don't know how you do it Jaz. You've got more things going on in one business than I ever thought possible." Lisa turned to Carrie. "I finally had to end my contracts with all my other bookkeeping clients because the Jazzy Clothing Company takes up all my time right now. *And* it was a push to just get my stuff done before we left!"

"All the stuff you do sounds so complicated! I just post stuff for sale, ship it after it sells, and let the accounting software Jonathan helped me set up do all the bookkeeping for me!"

Lisa smiled. "And you have your own beautiful success story out of it. I went on to your site the other day to see what Lauren had for sale. Every single thing was sold already!"

"It's a thing I learned from an art marketing blog! I used to pull listings as soon as they sold, but leaving them up for a week with a sold stamp over them really makes the new listings sell faster! I'll put up a few more of her things after camp. Let's make sure you look at them when we get home, and then if you want something I'll sell it to you directly."

"Deal! Now you and I need to stop talking shop, and hopefully Jaz will take a cue from us."

"I agree. So, what are you the most excited about at camp?"

Lisa laughed. "I can't believe after all these years I'll finally have my own summer camp memories!"

CHAPTER 16

"It looks like this is it," Lisa said as she put on her signal. They had been driving along a rural two-lane road for about twenty minutes, and now the sign saying 'Willow Lake Retreat' was a welcome sight.

"Ahhh," Carrie said, "I can feel myself relaxing already!"

"What, you didn't find my driving relaxing?" Lisa joked.

"Uh, there's running water, right?" Jaz asked from the backseat.

"I don't know Jaz. Mom didn't tell me anything about the place. She wanted it to be a surprise. For all I know we have to pee in the forest."

"You'd better be joking."

Lisa laughed, "Of course I'm joking! Haven't you ever been in the woods before?" She slowly drove down the winding lane.

"We did some nature walks when I was in elementary school. And then my mom would spend an hour looking for ticks before she let me in the house—oh."

They drove into a clearing where a moderate conference center-type building welcomed them. Huge containers of bright red and white flowers were set all along the gravel parking lot indicating individual spots. To the side facing a picture-perfect lake was a long balcony with polished Adirondack chairs begging for them to sit down and stretch out their legs.

The three of them got out and turned around slowly, taking in the birds singing and the gentle sound of water meeting the shore underneath a clear blue sky.

"Look! Look over there!" Jaz said in a stage whisper. At the edge of the woods a deer was standing and nibbling on the manicured lawn. "Will it chase us? Are we safe?"

"We're totally fine," Carrie answered without whispering. "The only thing she'll do is run away if we get too close."

"How do you know it's a girl?"

Lisa and Carrie exchanged glances. "Boys have antlers," Lisa answered. "I think you and Alex need to spend a little more time in the big outdoors."

Before Jaz could answer another car slowly drove into sight and parked right beside them. Kara, Lauren, and Jenny stepped out.

"Holy cow!" Lauren hollered. "This place is like a freaking painting! I love it!"

They all exchanged hugs and then followed Lisa to the main entrance. A man in his twenties wearing khaki shorts and a baby blue polo shirt with the center's logo on it opened the door for them. Lauren elbowed Lisa and Jaz and raised her eyebrows.

"Good afternoon ladies, welcome to Willow Lake Retreat. You must be the moms summer camp group!"

"We are," Lisa answered.

"Wonderful, let's get you checked in and then I'll take your luggage to your room for you. Oh, my name's Hank. I'm here if you have any questions and I'll also be leading a few nature walks that you have booked."

Jaz shuddered. "I might pass on those."

He stopped and looked at her with a huge smile. "You just give me one walk and I promise you'll be hooked. Don't worry, you're completely safe with me. OK ladies, this is Myrah, she handles all the administration here and the bookings. Myrah, meet the moms summer camp group."

As he stepped into a back office Lauren nudged Jaz again. "You'd better stay close to Mr. Perfectly Safe there city girl," she said jokingly.

"Uh, I plan on getting out of here alive. I don't think I'll leave that up to a stranger."

"Hank's a fully qualified medic and environmental educator," Myrah said with a smile. "You'll want to try at least one walk with him. Now, it looks like your coordinator has planned a wonderful week here for you all. I'll just take final payment from each of you and then you can relax for the rest of the week and let us take care of you."

A few minutes later they were following Hank and an overflowing luggage cart to the elevators. He sent them up first and then joined them on the second floor. Comfortable chairs and fresh flower arrangements were placed along the wide hallway.

"This is your room here, number two hundred. It's got one of my favorite views." He opened the door wide and stepped back so they could enter first.

The room was large with three bunk beds set up along the walls, a large sliding door that led onto the balcony, and a seating area with a small table.

"Bunk beds?" Jaz asked. "I've literally never slept in a bunk bed ... oh look! There's little gifts on each bed. Oh, they have names. Hey, where's mine?"

"I'm guessing you're on a top bunk," Kara said. "The old ladies get the bottom bunks."

Hank had wheeled the cart in and was unloading the luggage. "On the sideboard behind the table is a kettle and a coffee maker. You'll find extra supplies underneath. Just help yourself. There's also a few different kinds of hot chocolate and some instant soups, but our chef is pretty amazing, so leave lots of room for her cooking. I'll leave you to get settled in, but I'll be back in about half an hour to give you a tour."

They called their thank you's and started to find their beds.

"Wait a minute," Jenny said. "These gift bags are from Maria personally, not the center! Oh, too cute, she gave me a 'Baby On Board' pin and a little note that says, 'wear this every day to get the special treatment you deserve'. Well, I think my belly is starting to speak for itself, but I'll wear it anyways."

Each of them had received a few thoughtful gifts from Maria and a personal note.

"I have to say, Mom's been crazy happy planning all this. I think it's given her a virtual holiday!"

Jenny was the first to use the bathroom. "Wow, it's like a spa in there! We may have to make a schedule so all of us get a chance to use it. It really will feel like summer camp if we're lining up to use the bathroom!"

"At least there's the double sinks out here. That will help. And I love the fresh flowers everywhere!" Carrie lay down on her bed. "And somehow this bunk bed mattress is *really* comfortable!"

"It feels like a fort up here!" Jaz said. She was sitting on her bunk cross legged. "There's this cute little shelf for a book and a glass of water—it literally says that! Oh! And I can see the lake from up here!" She scrambled down, and went and opened the sliding doors.

CHAPTER 17

They all walked onto the balcony and looked out onto the lake. An island in the center had an inviting picnic table and small beach. On the shore near them, a dock led out into the water with a cozy arrangement of chairs at the end. To their left was a building with canoes and paddleboards stacked beside life jackets. To their right was a gazebo, and beside that a firepit with benches arranged in a circle around it.

"Do you think we'll have s'mores? I've never had s'mores before!" Jaz said excitedly.

Everyone turned to stare at her.

"What? You mean you've all had s'mores? I thought that was just a movie thing. OK, fine. I've kind of never done anything like this before OK? Go easy on me!"

Carrie went and put an arm around Jaz. "And here I thought I was missing out because I didn't go to camp. Yeah Jaz. S'mores are a real thing and Alex's life will be better because you're going to learn how to make them this week!"

"Wow," Lauren said, turning back to the view. "I feel like just looking at all of this is a therapy session. The colors. Even just all the different greens in one scene is amazing. I'm gonna be so ready to paint when I get back."

"Do you know what I love?" Kara asked. "Listen. You can't hear a single kid yelling. No doors slamming. No video games. And nobody is yelling 'mom'. Bliss."

"I can holler 'mom' once in a while if you want," Lisa offered. "Oh, wait, I've got something." She went back into the room and opened a box that Hank had brought in with the luggage. "Let's see, there should be glasses… Yep!"

A few minutes later she was back with a tray full of drinks. "Mom sent a cheat sheet, so … Jaz, the pink fizzy stuff is yours. Sparkling rosé I think. Kara, the beer is yours and the Coke is for you Lauren. Jenny that champagne flute is for you. It's organic sparkling grape juice. And Carrie and I both have Pinot Grigio." She set the tray down on one of the chairs. "Cheers ladies!"

They toasted each other and then turned back to the view. "How did your mom do this?" Lauren asked.

Lisa shrugged, "Beats me. But it's a good thing she sent a note with what to serve everyone!"

"What's wrong Lauren?" Carrie asked.

Lauren wiped away tears. "She went to all this work. For me. To know I don't have to say I'll just have water when everyone else is drinking. No one's ever done that for me before."

Carrie and Lisa both hugged Lauren from either side. "Well you deserve it," Carrie said. They all stood in silence for a while, taking in the view, enjoying the peace around them and the friendship between them.

"I know!" Jaz said suddenly. "Let's take pictures of us enjoying all the things that Maria's set up for us, and then we can do an album for her as a thank you!"

"She'll love that!" Lisa answered. "If we can make sure at least one of us gets a picture of everything, I can set up a shared photo account when we get back home so we can send them all there."

"If we had WiFi or phone service we could do it now," Jaz said pointedly.

"This will be good for all of us. Especially you. Otherwise you'd be working by the end of the day, and trying to rope me into working by tomorrow!"

"Not true," Jaz said, and then paused. "Well, maybe true. But we can't exactly find out now, can we?"

There was a knock at the door. "Tour time!" Jenny said after she answered. They all filed out to follow Hank.

"Wait!" Jaz called. "Shouldn't we lock the door?"

Hank turned around. "It's up to you. For today you're the only group here, and then tomorrow there's a group of a dozen women coming for a business retreat." He pointed up. "We do have CCTV monitoring the public areas, so it's pretty secure. But your room keys are in a bowl on the sideboard — I'll wait if you want to go get them."

"Oh. No. That's OK." Jaz answered.

Hank beamed. "See? You're relaxing already! Now, follow me. Here's an ice machine and a vending machine. At the other end of this hallway is a fully stocked library and sitting room. We'll go down the stairs here."

At the bottom of the stairs he opened a door that led to the part of the grounds they couldn't see from their room.

"Over here is the hot tub. You're welcome to use it anytime between six am and midnight. There's no glass permitted in this area, but you'll find stainless coffee mugs and unbreakable drink glasses in the dining room. Quite a few people enjoy having their coffee or tea here in the mornings. And it's a great place to relax after swimming in the lake, too."

He took them around to the outdoor activity area, the gazebo and campfire (where he assured Jaz that they provided s'mores fixings on request) and an outdoor eating area that led directly into the dining room.

Already smells of dinner were wafting through from the kitchen. "There's always beverages available here. According to our notes, none of you have any dietary requests … Sorry, we must have made an error. Can I get a list of those so I can get it to chef right away?"

They all looked at each other.

"Wait a minute. Six of you can eat everything? Whoa. That might be a first. Wild! I'll be right back." He jogged to the kitchen and returned a minute later. "Cool. OK. I'll just show you the spa and the chapel. Follow me."

Sure enough, there was a full-on spa with six pedicure chairs and three separate massage rooms. The chapel was a tiny non-denominational space offering a serene place that was welcoming to everyone.

"You may have noticed we don't have a gym or a yoga studio," he said and Lauren snickered. "But we do offer yoga on the beach every morning at 6:30. Just put your name down on the list at the registration desk the night before if you want to join the next day. We've got mats so all you have to bring is yourself and your water bottle. Other than that, if you want more activity in your day there's all the water sports and some great running or walking trails."

"OK, the last thing to go over is your schedule. It's back at the registration desk."

They exchanged glances as they followed him back down the hallway. "I was kind of counting on no schedule," Kara admitted. "With my life right now I practically have to schedule in time to go to the bathroom if I want it in my day!"

"Here you go," Hank said proudly, lifting up a small whiteboard that was sitting on the counter. "Your coordinator asked that we only give you the day's plan. It's an awesome way to live in the moment and not worry about tomorrow."

"We've got an intro to canoeing in half an hour. And then... massages? Really?" Lauren looked up from the board. "That'll be a first."

"There are three therapists coming in. I do apologize that we can't accommodate you all at once. But you're welcome to relax in the hot tub before or after, or take a little time in the chapel. Sherry will meet you at the boat shed soon. If you need anything at any time please dial zero from your room phone, or just ring the buzzer here and someone will be right with you. Enjoy your stay, ladies!"

"I'm beginning to question leaving my mom in charge of planning!" Lisa said. "What's the deal with keeping the rest of the week a secret?"

"She knows us too well," Carrie said. "We're all used to planning ahead and scheduling everything. This way we have no choice but to relax and go with the flow. It'll be fun!"

Lauren and Jaz both eyed her suspiciously. "Is this another one of your rosy happy things?" Lauren asked.

"Well, all I know about summer camp is from books and movies," she answered. "But it does seem to be a thing to have someone else in charge."

"I'm going to take charge here and say we all go relax on the balcony in front of that gorgeous view until our intro to canoeing." Jenny announced.

They all agreed and made their way back upstairs.

"So," Lisa asked as they all sat with their heads back and their legs stretched out in the afternoon sun. "How long until you stop thinking about all the things you should be doing and start relaxing?"

"Probably a lifetime," Kara quipped, "but I'm going to do my best to be a good camper anyways."

"When was your first camping experience?" Carrie asked.

They spent a relaxing half hour sharing memories of childhood summers before making their way down to the boat shed.

"I can't believe none of us have ever been in a canoe!" Jenny said. "In the past I've always been surrounded by a bunch of people who have been everywhere and done everything. I guess I've finally found my tribe!"

The next hour was full of laughter—most of it genuine, some of it nervous. They all managed to get in and out of the canoes without capsizing, although there was a lot of wobbling.

Eventually they all paddled out in a group and managed to turn around and get back to shore without incident. They tumbled out of their boats, laughing and high-fiving each other on their successful voyage.

Sherry encouraged them to take the canoes out again in the evening so they could enjoy watching the sunset from the water. "Since you're the only group here tonight, feel free to leave your life jackets in the canoes. But tomorrow I'll ask you to return them to the hooks when you're done."

They all thanked her and made their way to the spa. Jenny, Lauren, and Lisa would go first for massages, since Carrie, Jaz, and Kara all wanted to try out the hot tub first. It had cooled off a little while they were on the lake, making it a tempting option.

Two and a half hours later they made their way to the dining room for supper.

"I'm crazy starving!" Lauren said. "And whatever that smell is, it's making me cross-eyed."

The chef was waiting for them, "Hello! You're my very first group of I-can-eat-anything diners, so it's been extra wonderful to cook for you. Tonight we're featuring a bourbon orange glazed ham with house made coleslaw, crispy smashed potatoes, and fresh rosemary rolls. We serve cafeteria style here, so feel free to head over and fill your plates. When you're done, please bring all your dishes to the table over here. If you need anything, please pop your head in the kitchen and let me know!"

Lauren was the first in line. She paused after picking up her plate and looked over the little group. "In case I haven't been clear, I officially love Mom's Camp and I never want to leave!"

Soon they were exclaiming over the food and trying to decide if they could replicate the dishes at home.

CHAPTER 18

"This is so weird," said Lauren. She was sitting with the other moms on the balcony with her feet up on the railing. A second cup of coffee was in her hand. "I can't wait to see Dustin and Brittany and be home. And... I don't want to leave here. Ever."

"You describe it perfectly." Jenny was rubbing her stomach and holding a mug with hot water and lemon. "This has been such a perfect getaway. I have to admit, when I saw the bunkbeds and realized we were all sharing a room I was pretty disappointed. But we would've missed out on so many good things if we were separated!"

"I never had any girlfriends when I was growing up," Lisa started, "so I guess I didn't think this week would be much of anything except getting some extra sleep and maybe enjoying nature. But now I just have this crazy deep appreciation for all of you, and I really thank you all for giving my mom full rein to plan it!"

Jaz stood up and leaned over the railing. "That album is going to be epic! And now I can't wait to take Alex out into the woods and stuff."

"Are you going to call Hank?" Lauren asked.

"What do you mean?"

"We all saw him give you his phone number!"

"Oh. Nope. Totally not my type," she said with a firm voice.

Lisa looked at the watch she had put on for the first time that morning. "I hate to break up the party, but I think we need to be on our way." There was a knock at the door. "That'll be Hank to take our luggage down."

They all got up reluctantly and decided to take the stairs down after Hank had collected their luggage. Outside they distributed everything between the two cars, and then stalled as long as they could.

"Shoot!" Jenny said. "Need one more bathroom break!" She ran inside and they all said goodbye one more time before getting into the cars. When Jenny came back they drove away slowly.

"Well," Lisa said as she turned onto the main road, "make sure you say a huge thank you to Jonathan for coming up with this Mom Camp idea. Now that I've been, I can honestly say every mom should have this to look forward to."

"Maybe our next project should be to set up a scholarship fund so more moms can go!" Carrie said half-jokingly.

"But it was our friendships that made it what it was," Jaz pointed out.

They all agreed. Lisa touched a few buttons and the sounds of nature filled the car.

"Nice," Carrie gave a thumbs up. "Keeps the nature thing going. Wow, music sure is easier to hear in *your* car. By the way, Katie doesn't like it because it's *too* quiet."

"Yeah, that would be my only complaint about an electric car too. But can you imagine how much more peaceful our cities would be if every vehicle was this quiet."

"Not to mention how much cleaner!" Jaz said, leaning forward between the two front seats. "Dad said we need to look at our company's carbon footprint to see—oh, sorry. Work talk."

"Yeah, how do we re-enter our worlds after a week like that? Quick like ripping off a band-aid, or slowly so we don't traumatize ourselves?"

"However it happens I think I'm way more set to keep calm going forward. I feel like I had forgotten how to relax. With Alex so busy and always trying to work when he doesn't need me, it's been a long time since I stopped for a while and smelled the roses."

"Well, the roses I planted in my back yard are blooming like crazy, so come on over any time and smell them," Lisa offered.

When she pulled onto Carrie's street she took a deep breath. "Here we go ladies! Back to craziness!"

As soon as she pulled into the driveway the door opened and Katie came out as fast as she could, considering she was holding Alex's hand. They were both shouting 'Mommy!'

Carrie and Jaz both stopped and Lisa went straight inside to look for Marcus.

Soon they were all inside catching up on hugs, stories, and laughter. Marcus kept looking at Lisa's face and squealing with joy.

"Well," Jonathan said, "thanks to Mom and Dad we survived. But only just. I've been counting the hours until you all got home. I swear, Carrie, even Maisy got all mopey while you were gone!"

"Aw," Carrie said, crouching down to give Maisy some more scratches. "Thanks for missing me Maisy!" The puppy put her paws on Carrie's knee and almost got a lick in before Carrie moved her face away. "Still no licks though thank you very much." She stood up and Katie wrapped her arms around her waist.

"I liked having everyone here, but I like having you here best, Mommy."

"Aw, thanks Katie-girl! I like being here best too but I sure loved Mommy Camp!"

"Well, I want to get home," Lisa said as she cuddled Marcus. "Jaz are you ready to go?"

Jonathan stepped forward and picked up the portable cot Marcus had been sleeping in, "Here, let me help you load the car. Kudos on getting this all in on the way over by the way!"

Soon they were driving away, and Carrie gratefully sank into the couch. "I'm glad you're staying 'til tomorrow," she said to her parents. "At least we'll have a chance to spend some time together this evening."

"So," she said to Katie, "tell me everything." And that's exactly what Katie proceeded to do. "I feel like I didn't miss out on anything! Thanks!"

"You did miss out on the constant demands of babies," Jonathan said. "Your mom was either holding a baby or dealing with a kid the entire week."

"I loved it," she smiled. "Every minute of it."

"And what about you Dad? Did you do much diaper duty?"

"Well, I really enjoyed my time with Dustin every day. That man is a walking miracle, and quite funny when you get used to the way he talks. Other than that... Matthew and I might have gone out on a few really long errands," he admitted sheepishly.

"You and Matthew are a lot alike that way. You both prefer solitude or small groups over mass chaos! I'm glad you found a way to survive."

She turned to Jonathan. "Any news about the application?"

He shook his head. "Still nothing."

"It's going to work out Care Bear," her mom said, using her childhood nickname. "I know it's hard to wait. Especially because your little one is out there somewhere right now. But the timing is going to make perfect sense in retrospect. Enjoy your first summer as a family, get lots of sleep, and try not to worry."

"Will I be as wise as you when I'm your age Mom?"

"Oh, you're already wiser than me. You just don't know it yet."

"It's good advice," Jonathan admitted. "I was actually wondering if you all would be interested in going to the coast together to see Jessica next month. We could take a couple days and drive there, or all fly together. I already checked. There are some accessible Airbnb's we could rent. We could even find one big enough for Jessica to stay in, too."

Carrie looked at Jonathan. That man was full of surprises. "When did you come up with this?"

"Your mom has been talking a lot to Katie about Auntie Jessica. It's clear you all miss her. And it sounds like it's still nearly impossible for her to get more than a day or two off at a time. So this seems like the best idea. Plus, I got an unexpected payment from a client a few months ago and your daughter here," he tipped his head towards Carrie, "is, quite frankly, terrible at spending money. So we can easily cover the cost."

"Well," her dad said slowly, "that's quite an offer. We'd need to give it some thought. Coming here is one thing. We know how everything's set up and it's perfect for Julia. But travelling further? We've never done that before."

"There's no pressure," Jonathan assured them.

"Speaking of pressure," Julia said, "I think I need to lay down for a while."

"I'll help you, Mom," Carrie started to get up.

"Nope. I've been practicing and I can do it all myself. You can come relax with me though."

Carrie watched in awe as her mom lowered the platform at the bottom of the stairs, wheeled her chair onto it, locked it in, and then rode up the stairs. At the other end she wheeled off, raised the platform back up to its storage position, and made her way into the guest room. Once there, she used the frame installed over the bed to transfer herself.

Then she giggled. "Well, I can almost do it all! Care Bear, there's the small issue of the blankets I seem to have forgotten to turn down first."

"Well, I'm glad you need me for *something*," Carrie joked as she carefully adjusted her mom's position so she could pull out the blankets.

"Just the light one please. The temperature's always perfect in here."

When she was sure her mom was comfortable and didn't have any clothes or bedding bunched underneath her, Carrie climbed on the other side and found the position she had mastered as a little girl after the accident that changed their lives forever. She lay on her side with her head on her mom's shoulder and gently held her mom's hand in hers.

"Tell me the truth Mom, how did it all go?"

"Well, Alex is a little firecracker to be sure. He got into everything he could get his hands on, and a few things we thought were out of his reach. But every time Jonathan responded with such patience. It was really lovely to see. And, of course, Katie does what she sees, so she became quite the little helper!" She chuckled. "Maisy learned to just stay away from him."

"And how were the other kids?"

"We only had Angela and Marcus two of the days, since Max managed to get an extra day off. It was fine. At that point there was always enough kids to entertain each other and our job was feeding and bathrooms. Matthew really liked Marcus but I think Alex and Brittany were a bit much for him. They adored him, of course, but they both wanted to climb on him all the time."

"Mmmm, I'll have to remember that when we get our next child. It would probably be easier for Matthew if they were a bit older."

"Don't you worry about the right fit. It will become clear when the time's right."

"You sound like some sort of sage or something."

"Maybe I am," she replied with a hint of laughter.

CHAPTER 19

Carrie felt like she just blinked her eyes and it was the second week of school. They had taken her mom's advice and enjoyed their first summer together as a family, as well as ferried the kids to camps, events, and friend's places.

Their trip to Jessica had ended up being a last-minute decision when she called to say she had three days off in a row the following week. They divided the drive into two days so Carrie's mom wasn't sitting too long without a break, and enjoyed three days of exploring the city with Jessica as their guide.

There had just been enough time to get the kids ready for school when they got back, and now Carrie and Jonathan were parents of an eighth grader and a third grader.

"Does the shock of the kids getting older ever wear off?" Jonathan asked after they dropped Katie off at her new classroom.

"Nope. And remember, when our kids are older we're older."

"Yeah. I definitely feel that today. I wish Matthew would have wanted us to drop him off, too. Starting high school is scary!"

"Well, they did a lot of transition activities in the spring," Carrie reminded him. "And he knows at least fifty kids from elementary school. He'll be fine. I hope."

"I guess all that's left is for us to get a phone call telling us we've passed part one of the adoption application and they're ready to start the homestudy." His phone rang, and both he and Carrie looked at each other hopefully. "Hello? Oh, yes, hi. I'm glad it worked out for you…"

Carrie tuned out the rest of the conversation when she realized it was business. Instead, her thoughts turned to her own work. Alicia had continued to meet with Carrie throughout the summer and was beginning to come to terms with her new single life. Brian wasn't interested in any counseling together, and had come by a few days in a row when Alicia was at work to remove most of his belongings.

It was a stark reality for Alicia to look around the house she thought she'd share with Brian and only see her own things. But she was taking Carrie's suggestions to heart, and focusing her energy on reframing her life to fit her new, more positive, and more giving outlook on life.

Alicia had referred two other women she'd met through an online IVF support group to Carrie, which left her busier than she had expected. Plus, in another two months she hoped to have her provisional status removed and become fully licensed as a counseling psychologist. It would only result in a small raise at the clinic, but it was a title she was excited to hold, nonetheless.

"You look lost in thought."

It took Carrie a moment to realize Jonathan was talking to her and not his client on the phone. "What? Oh, I didn't know you were done. Yeah, thinking about my own clients and how they're progressing—or not—as the case may be."

"I always tell you, the long ones mean job security!"

"Ha ha. So—" His phone rang again.

"Hello, Jonathan Brandt here. Oh, yes!" He grabbed Carrie's arm and shook it. "We are? That's great news! ... Of course, Carrie's right here ... Start the homestudy on September fourteenth?"

Carrie quickly unlocked her phone and checked her schedule. She did have clients that day, but she'd work them around the appointment. She nodded and gave Jonathan a thumbs up.

"Yes, that works for us ... No, that's a tiny bit earlier than we can manage with getting kids to school. This is without the kids, correct? ... Sure, eight thirty is fine ... Great! We'll see you then!" He ended the call and then picked up Carrie and spun her around. "We did it! We passed the first test!"

"Seriously? Just like that they tell us? I can't believe it!"

"Believe it, baby!"

"Wait, what do we do now? I mean, should we clean the house and practice our answers or something? It's a big deal!"

"Carrie, we need to just be ourselves and let them see us as we really are."

"Right. You're right." She took a deep breath. "It's huge though. The whole thing. Let's hurry home and tell everyone."

In some ways, it felt like announcing a pregnancy—but one without a due date, or any physical signs. They called all their friends and family, received well wishes from everyone, and then acknowledged that they still somehow had to get through the next thirteen days until their homestudy began.

When the day finally arrived, they had spent so much time reassuring the kids that they almost believed this was 'just the next step'. Only it wasn't. It was someone who was probably trained to spot dysfunctional families coming into their home and evaluating everything. As far as they knew, even the darkest corners of the basement and garage might be inspected.

When the doorbell rang, Carrie had to wipe her sweaty hands on her pants before she could open the door.

A social worker with a bouncy ponytail who couldn't be older than twenty was standing there with a laptop bag over her shoulder. "Hi!" she said. "I'm Sophie! I'm here to conduct your adoption homestudy!"

Carrie held out her hand. "Sophie, hi, I'm Carrie, and this is my husband Jonathan." She stepped aside after shaking Sophie's hand to let her in. Jonathan shook her hand as well.

"Wow, you guys have a gorgeous home! And what a great neighborhood! I love the playground just down the street—oh, hello!" She reached down and let Maisy sniff her. "You're probably smelling my little doggies! They're named Popo and Momo!"

She stood up, "They're Pomeranians. What's your dog?"

"Well, Maisy came from a stray momma that the shelter rescued so we really have no idea! Um, where would you like to start?"

"Why don't you show me around your house and then we'll settle at the table for a chat?" She set her bag down and pulled out a tablet. "Do you mind if I take pictures? It helps me remember everything later when I write the report."

"Go ahead!"

The first thing she noticed was the wheelchair lift. "My mom's in a wheelchair," Carrie explained, "so the house is set up so she can visit whenever she wants."

They went through each room, with Sophie taking dozens of pictures. Finally they were back at the table where she put away her tablet and pulled out a laptop.

"Can I get you something to drink?" Jonathan asked. "Coffee, tea, water?"

"Oh, just a glass of water would be nice."

"It's nice that you can take your notes with a computer," Carrie said, trying to make conversation.

"Well, believe it or not, I still have to fill out the final report on paper. Our area's pretty behind in the technology department, so although I have quite the procedure to follow to be able to use my personal devices, at least I can. Some other states are fully online with the application, and it makes it way faster."

"I'll bet," Jonathan said as he brought three glasses of water to the table.

"So," Sophie started, "I know you've filled out a gazillion questions about adopting, but I'd like you to tell me in your own words why you want to adopt and what you expect from adoption."

Two hours later Carrie felt like she had unloaded her entire soul to Sophie. She may have looked young, but she had a knack for asking questions that demanded in-depth answers.

"Now, there's just one more thing to cover. Two years ago there was a police call to your house Carrie, because of a domestic disturbance. Can you tell me about that?"

Carrie was shocked that they had that information, and it took her a minute to be able to speak. "At the time I was single, and I had a teenage girl living with me who was pregnant. My ex-husband, Don, had been in jail because of a drinking and driving conviction—four of them, actually." She closed her eyes, trying not to get too emotional as she remembered the terror of that day. Under the table, Jonathan gently took her hand.

"I had a little bit of warning that Don was probably out of jail and looking for me. He wasn't supposed to be out for a few more months, but you know how they seem to let a lot of people out early."

Sophie nodded sympathetically.

"I happened to see him pull up just as I was about to take the kids swimming. So I sent them out the back door to go get help from Jonathan. We weren't dating at the time, but he lived less than a block away and I knew he was home renovating his house. This house actually."

"Anyways, my plan was to ignore Don. He was pounding on the door and yelling for me to bring the kids. And then all of a sudden I could hear him yelling awful, racist stuff and I knew that Jaz had come home—she's Chinese. I opened the door because I was afraid he'd hurt Jaz.

"I tried to send him away but he refused to leave. Jaz dialed 911 right away, and shortly after that Jonathan came running down the sidewalk. I didn't know it at the time, but another one of our good friends was helping him at the house, so Jonathan had the kids stay there and he ran over here."

"Once there was a big guy standing over him, Don decided to leave. But I knew there was no way he was supposed to be driving so we reported his license as he drove off. It was terrifying for me, but even worse for Jaz. She had never been yelled at like that before. I guess the good thing is that the kids didn't see any of it."

"And how much interaction does Don have with the kids now?" Sophie asked.

Carrie tried not to be worried about the speed Sophie was typing as she talked. "The kids currently have court-ordered supervised visits with him. It's supposed to be every month for two hours, but he doesn't always show up. Jonathan and I always drop the kids off and wait in the parking lot, hoping that this is one of the times he doesn't show up."

"What do the kids say about it?"

"Well, at thirteen years old Matthew could refuse to go and the courts wouldn't push it. But he knows that that would leave Katie there alone with Don, so he goes every time."

"I'm sorry, I thought you said they were supervised."

"Right. Yes, they are, but Don's very manipulative so it helps to have Matthew there. According to one of the social workers, he'll just come out and say 'that's not true' when Don tries to say something bad about me or Jonathan. I know that the supervisor can't exactly step in every time Don opens his mouth."

"Ah. I see. It sounds like you're in a difficult situation there, but you're doing everything you can to manage it. Has Don ever come to this house?"

"No," Jonathan answered. "We've got security cameras outside the house that track everyone who comes and goes. He hasn't been here."

"That's good. Well, it's been wonderful talking to you both. And I can't wait to meet Matthew and Katie!" She closed her laptop and put it away, and then pulled out a bundle of papers clipped together. "What I have here is a checklist about all sorts of home safety things that we require for foster parents. When we place a child for adoption, there's a three month time frame when they're still considered wards of the state. During this time you must comply with all the same standards as a foster parent. I'd like you to get started on these so when I come back I can verify that everything's good."

Next, she took out her phone, "Alright. The next thing to do is schedule a time to come back when I can chat with the whole family. I don't need to be alone with the kids. In fact, I really don't like pulling kids away from their parents, but it's very important that they be allowed to answer every question themselves without input from Mom and Dad. Is that something you can manage?"

Jonathan and Carrie looked at each other.

"I think your challenge will be getting Katie to *stop* talking!" he said with an affectionate smile. "Matthew needs a bit more time to answer questions, but Carrie's done an amazing job of teaching Katie to let Matthew have his time to talk without interruptions."

"It nearly kills her," Carrie said with a chuckle, "but she can do it."

"Wonderful. Is there an afternoon next week when you're all at home?"

"We don't have any activities until the evening on Tuesdays and Fridays."

"OK, let's do Friday at three thirty. And I promise to be out of your hair by five thirty so you can make it to your activities." She put the date into her phone and stood up. "It's been great to meet you!"

A minute later she was out the door and Carrie was in Jonathan's arms. "I sure didn't expect her to bring up that stuff with Don. Are you alright?"

Carrie nodded, "I just need a minute here." They stood there holding each other. Eventually she took a few deep breaths and stepped back. "We did it! We made it through the first part of the homestudy!"

"You were wonderful Mrs. Brandt."

"And *you* were wonderful Mr. Brandt."

CHAPTER 20

"And Mommy said that I might get a new brother *or* a new sister so I just say sister-brother whenever I'm talking about them so I don't leave anyone out. I wanted them to sleep in my room when they come, but Mommy said they need to have their own space. But they can play in my room whenever they want!" Her face fell. "Well, unless they're like baby Alex. He's two and he messes up everything. If my brother-sister is like Alex then I'll need to keep my door shut." Her face brightened. "But I could bring my stuffies into their room and play with them! Stuffies are hard to break."

"That's a very good idea! I can see that you've been thinking a lot about your sister-brother. Is there anything that worries you about adopting?"

"Wellllll …"

Carrie and Jonathan looked at each other, wondering what she could possibly come up with.

"I was telling my class about you today. And how we were going to maybe hopefully adopt a sister-brother. Then at recess one of the mean boys came over and said adopted kids always burn down houses and run away."

"And then what did you do?" Sophie asked.

"I told him that wasn't true! But is it true Miss Sophie? Do adopted kids do bad stuff like that?"

"Well Katie, many adopted kids have gone through some rough stuff. And sometimes they do act out. But I can tell you that in all my years of being a social worker I haven't heard of a single house fire."

"Oh! That's good. I *knew* it wasn't true!"

"I'd like to ask Matthew some questions now. Would you like to go play or watch TV?"

Katie pointed at the wall mounted TV. "I don't think I should watch while you're talking to Matthew. That's our only TV. I know! I can go get the stuffies that I want to share with my sister-brother and you can tell me which ones are good!"

"That's a great idea! But if I'm still talking with Matthew when you come back down could you try to be super quiet? I take notes better when everything's quiet so I can listen carefully."

"Yep! Bye!" Katie shouted and ran upstairs to her room.

"So Matthew, what's your favorite thing to do in your free time?" Sophie asked.

"Um … pretty much play guitar. And my Dad and I play some video games. That's fun. I have some friends. We bike around or play video games."

"How do you think another child will impact you?"

He looked at Carrie and she hoped she had a neutral expression. If Matthew had any concerns, she wanted to know about them.

"I … a long time ago my mom was really sad. I think, like, I know these kids might be kinda rough, and I think I can be patient. But I'm a little worried that they might make my mom sad."

"And what might happen then?"

"Well, I guess Jonathan would fix it. I mean, the last time mom was sad we didn't even know Jonathan. So that's good now. And Katie's really good at making us all laugh—she's not trying or anything, she's just kinda crazy in a funny way—so that would help too."

"What about the extra time and energy that another child would take?"

"Yeah, I've thought about that. The thing is, even though Mom had that sad time, we've been really lucky. Like, we've always had each other, and we've always had a house, and food. And my parents are both really good with money so we can pay for another child. Like, I think we should share what we have."

"Geez, you've *really* been thinking about this, haven't you?" Sophie sounded a little bit emotional.

"Yeah. I do a lot of thinking. My mom's helping me be careful about what I think so I try to stick to thinking about good stuff."

"Matthew, would it be OK if I shared some of the things you've said with other social workers? Without saying your name or anything? I think it would really encourage them to know there are kids right now who are so socially conscious and aware of the opportunity to share what they have with others."

"Uh, yeah. But it's not just me. My friends think the same way. It's not like their parents are applying to adopt or anything. But yeah, we know we're lucky."

Sophie looked at Carrie and Jonathan. "Well done Mom and Dad. You've kept quiet the whole time! Any other concerns you have Matthew?"

"No. I'm good."

"Can I come down now?" Katie called from the top of the stairs where she had been watching through the railing.

"Of course," Sophie said with a huge smile. "Come introduce me to your stuffies!"

Sophie took another ten minutes talking stuffies with Katie before turning back to Carrie and Jonathan. "Are you ready to review the home safety checklist or do you need more time?"

"We're ready!"

"Great, let's go through it one item at a time."

After they had satisfied Sophie that their home was safe in every way, she gave them one more set of papers. "This is the last step. Blood tests for both of you. There will be a cost for this, but keep your receipts as adoption expenses are tax deductible. I must be on my way. Now my job is to put this all together and send it on to my supervisor. You can expect to hear from us two to three weeks after you submit the blood test results."

"And then what happens?" Jonathan asked.

"Well, once your application is approved, your file will be transferred to an adoption worker. This is a social worker who's really your voice. Their job will be matching you with the right child for your family. And then if you do get matched, they'll partner with you for the transition, at which point you'll switch social workers *again* and that child's social worker becomes your worker as well."

"Wow. The system has more layers than seven layer bean dip!" he joked.

"Way more! And some days it doesn't taste so good. But we're here for the kids. So that makes it all worth it. Well, I'd better be on my way. I'm so glad I got to know you all!"

"Bye Miss Sophie! I hope you're taking good care of my sister-brother until they come!"

Sophie paused with her hand on the doorknob. She turned and crouched down to look Katie in the eye. "I hope so too, Katie."

CHAPTER 21

At the beginning of November a terrified Max called to say that Jenny was in labour. Jonathan and Carrie dropped everything to head over to their house, leaving Matthew to watch Katie.

Jenny greeted them at the door, looking like she should fall over from the weight of her belly on her thin frame. She rested a hand on her lower back as she held the door open. "It's early days right now you guys. You really didn't need to come so quickly."

They both did their best to hug her around her belly, and then followed her upstairs.

"Well," Carrie said, "if you don't need us maybe we can help keep Max from passing out."

He looked up from the couch where he was sitting with his head in his hands. "Just wait until you see her belly during a contraction. It's like watching an alien take over your wife's body."

Carrie made a sympathetic face. "Been there, done that. You just need to remember to breathe and focus on Jenny's face."

Jonathan looked back at Jenny. "Seriously? I thought it was bad enough watching junior try to punch through your stomach these past two months. Don't we have a way to make this easier? I mean, we've made it to the moon and all already!"

He was interrupted by Angela coming down the hallway. "Uncle Johnny!"

He reached down and picked her up, holding her in a long hug. "Hey Angel. I hear it might be the day you get to meet your sister or brother!"

Angela nodded. "I think Daddy's scared," she whispered.

"I think so too. We'll take good care of him, OK?"

She nodded and he put her down. "Hi Aunty Carrie," she said shyly.

Carrie crouched down and hugged her. "Hello! Katie is super excited that you're going to come over to our place. She even has a special big sister present to give you."

Angela's eyes widened. "She does?"

"Yep. And you can play in the living room and watch Daniel Tiger's Neighborhood." Angela was a quiet, sensitive child who had reverted back to her favorite toddler shows in the past few months. Carrie assured Max and Jenny that it was temporary, and once she got used to the changes in their family she'd probably lose interest in the show.

"You know, I really think it's going to be a while. You guys are welcome to head back home and we can drop Angela off on the way to the hospital." Jenny offered.

Jonathan shook his head. "Are you kidding? There's no way I could get anything done. I might as well stick around here and *we'll* drop Angel off when it's time. Besides, she likes my fancy car better than your old minivan, right Angel?"

"Yes," she said with a little smile.

"Now," Jonathan said, "they're probably going to be all 'baby' this and 'baby' that. Should we go play in your room for a while instead?"

"My playroom's all gone now because we need a baby's room."

"I heard. So, does that mean you actually get to have all your toys in your bedroom with you? All the time?"

Angela looked surprised. "But I don't have a playroom!"

He waved his hand in the air. "Playrooms are totally last year. I heard that all the cool kids have moved their toys into their bedrooms."

"You're silly Uncle Johnny," she giggled.

He reached out his hand to her. "You have to be silly too then. C'mon, skip to your bedroom with me!"

She skipped beside him while he pretended to trip over his feet and almost fall. The sound of her laughter was priceless.

Jenny gave Carrie a pointed look. "That man is worth his weight in gold right now."

"Hey," Max said weakly from the couch, "I'm right here."

"And you'll be worth your weight in gold too when you're changing diapers and doing nighttime feeds," she said, patting his head. "Carrie, coffee or tea for you?"

"Just water please," she said as she followed Jenny into the kitchen.

Jenny leaned into Carrie as she let the water run. "I'm so glad you're here," she said quietly. "Don't leave me until he can verify that baby and I aren't going to die on him."

"I thought you wanted us to leave!" Carrie whispered back.

"That was just for show. And I knew you wouldn't lea—" she gripped the counter with both hands and leaned forward as a low groan came out. In a second, Max was by her side.

He gave Carrie a panicky look as he rubbed Jenny's back. When the contraction passed, Jenny filled a glass and gave it to Carrie.

"Should you be doing that honey?" he asked.

Carrie put her arm through Max's and pulled him toward the living room. "This is going to come as a huge shock to you, but women have actually been doing this quite successfully for thousands of years. Give Jenny at least a little credit, will you?"

"I'm terrible, aren't I," he asked sheepishly.

"The worst," Carrie agreed. "But I heard a rumor that Jenny's going to keep you regardless. Lucky man."

The three of them spent the next two hours trying to distract Max so Jenny could have her contractions in peace. Jonathan and Angela joined them in the living room, and she was sitting on his lap, watching shows on her iPad.

Jenny was starting to pace during contractions. "Seriously?"

They all looked up to see her standing in a puddle of water.

"Mommy, I think you had an accident," Angela said in a very serious tone.

"Actually, it's the baby making the accident sweetie," Carrie answered. "I think Katie's waited long enough for you to come over. Can you go with Uncle Jonathan and get your things?"

"Yes, Daddy and I packed them a long time ago." She took Jonathan's hand. "We just have to remember my toothbrush and my special teddy and my school bag."

"It's a good thing you're so organized," he answered.

"Okey dokey. What do you want first, Jenny? Dry clothes or me to clean up?" Carrie decided to ignore Max, who was bent over hyper-ventilating, for the time being. At least he was sitting on the couch still. If he passed out he wouldn't have far to fall.

"Can you grab a towel from the linen closet to throw on this and help me change?" Jenny asked.

Ten minutes later Carrie was helping Max and Jenny into the mini-van. They agreed that Max was in no condition to drive, and Jenny shouldn't drive, so Carrie would take them to the hospital and Jonathan would follow after dropping off Angela.

"Make sure the house is locked up!" she called to him before buck-ling Max up. His hands were shaking. "Seriously dude, you need to pull it together here."

She winked at Jenny when she got into the driver's seat. Jenny had gotten herself and her hospital bag into the van without help.

When they arrived at the hospital Carrie decided to send Max in for the wheelchair. He seemed to perk up a little bit knowing it was a task he should be able to handle.

"Is he going to be OK?" Carrie asked Jenny as soon as he was out of earshot.

"Honestly? I'm not sure. He was totally fine when Angela came. In fact, he was amazing!" She groaned and breathed through a contrac-tion. "Carrie, I'm wondering if this is like a delayed reaction to me having cancer. He never expressed any worry the whole time. He was a total rock."

"Maybe," Carrie answered. "But he's going to have to get you and baby through labor and back home before he gets a turn to face his demons. Let me handle him if needed, OK? But maybe he'll snap out of this." She took in his very pale face as he pushed a wheelchair over, leaning heavily on the handles. *Or maybe not,* she thought to herself.

CHAPTER 22

"Dude! You've got two daughters!" Jonathan exclaimed, slapping his brother on the back.

"I do, don't I?" he said, still dazed and very pale.

Once Jenny was settled on the maternity ward the nurses had taken over, dealing with her *and* Max as needed. Carrie and Jonathan had done their best to help, and in the end Max was able to be with his wife as their second daughter was born.

"Is she OK?" Max asked. "Did you double check? Is she OK? Is the baby OK?"

The nurse who had been with them for the past hour overheard and came over to the chair he had been put in after the baby was born. "Listen Mr. Brandt. Everything is fine. More than fine. Everything is perfect. Your wife is an absolute rockstar. But now she needs you to knock off the worrying, OK?"

He nodded obediently.

"No, I mean it. You cannot get her all worried. Right now she's basking in the glow of a successful delivery and holding your perfect little daughter and I don't want you to take that away from her. Trust me, she may never forgive you if you do. So. Throw off all the worries right now. Are you done?"

"Yes ma'am."

"Good. Go in there and enjoy your wife and daughter."

He stood up, squared his shoulders, and went back into the room.

"Will he be alright now?" Carrie asked the nurse quietly.

"I'll be standing right behind him just in case," she said while following him in.

Carrie and Jonathan looked at each other and burst out laughing. They desperately needed a release from all the stress of the past few hours.

"Oh my gosh. That nurse deserves an award!"

Jonathan pulled out his phone, "I'm ordering cupcakes delivered for all the nurses on the ward. I'll sign the note from 'Max, the world's worst delivery partner'."

Carrie started laughing again when she realized Jonathan was serious.

A few minutes later Max walked out and invited them to come meet their niece, and they followed him into the room. "This is Brielle Carrie Brandt."

Carrie's mouth dropped open. "No way! Seriously?"

Jenny reached out her hand to Carrie. "First of all, you rescued me when I was at my worst. Then, you became my dearest friend. Then, you became my sister. I'll probably give all the rest of our kids the middle name Carrie."

Max paled. "We're doing this again?"

"Just wanted to check your hearing," Jenny smiled. "Thanks for not passing out on me today."

He carefully picked up Brielle and kissed her forehead. "Thanks for doing all the hard work and not divorcing me." They laughed and he looked up. "No, seriously. She should have kicked me to the curb today. I'm a lucky, lucky man."

CHAPTER 23

Carrie adjusted her earbuds and took a deep breath before clicking the link to connect. Her counseling sessions with Alicia were biweekly now, as she adjusted to the changes in her life.

"Hi Carrie!" Alicia's face popped up on the screen. She was almost unrecognizable from a few months ago.

"Hello! Wow! Are you somehow magnifying the sun there? I've never seen it so bright!"

Alicia looked behind her, "I know. Isn't it great! This is our third day in a row of all sun and no rain. I think it's a sign!"

"It helps, doesn't it? So, catch me up on where you are right now."

She paused, "Well, Brian sent me divorce papers last week. It was a shock, even though I knew they were coming. And you were right Carrie, about the money. He wants to keep way more than his fair portion." She gave a sad smile. "I missed so much work for IVF treatments and stress leave that my earnings are about twenty percent lower than prior years. I just assumed that was my loss, but my lawyer was saying how we made those decisions as a couple and I shouldn't hold the financial cost of that all by myself."

"You know," Alicia continued, "he always said the right words to be supportive, but this has shown another side of him that I really don't like. How could we have been equal partners when he was totally fine with me taking a huge drop in salary to have children?"

"So, do I hear you saying this new information is changing how you view the separation?" Carrie asked.

"Totally. Well, yes and no. I still love him, and I miss him a lot—although less than I used to. But I'm beginning to realize that what I loved more than him was this picture I had in my head of us as a family with kids. Like, seriously, *that* was what I wanted the most. Not him."

"That's exactly what we've been talking about, isn't it? How the pictures in our head represent our values and the things we actually want the most. OK. So, we've also talked about when your life doesn't match the picture you feel unhappy and unsatisfied. And you have the chance to choose to either change the picture of what you want, or change the things you've been doing to get what you want. Where are you at with that?"

"Yeah, I'm already doing that! Well, I'm trying. The picture of me, Brian, and kids is pretty strong. To change it to me, kids, and some other guy that I might be with in the future? That's hard, but I'm working on it. And when I take Brian out of the family picture it's easier to let go of him. Is that a sign of a totally dysfunctional marriage Carrie? That the only thing I wanted him for was kids?"

"Not at all! That's part of a life together with someone, when you realize that what you want isn't working and either needs to be changed, or worked on. In this case, the decision has already been made for Brian to leave. But if you were in a different relationship and you realized this, it would be an opportunity to strengthen your relationship as you addressed this new information."

Carrie paused to take a sip of water. "I'd like to know if there are other things—other pictures—in your Quality World—that's the mental place you hold all these pictures—that you've become aware of."

"I think that's what I need to work on. I feel like there are other things there, but I've been so crazy focused on having a baby and being a mom that I've ignored all those other things! I know my job is one of them. I actually don't always love being a paralegal, but I love that I paid my own way through school, got a good job, and I can support myself. So that's a big deal."

It was true. Without a good job, Alicia would be in a much worse financial situation right now, and that would impact everything else in her life. "That's great Alicia! Anything else?"

"Softball!"

"Pardon me?"

"I used to love playing softball. Our girls' high school team even made it to the championships, and after I graduated I always played in an adult rec league! It's just ... I played when Brian and I were dating and he came to all my games. But after we got married he quit coming and I started feeling guilty being there without him. So I eventually quit." She smirked. "And the only reason I remembered is because Brian wants to sell this house so I was trying to clean out my stuff and I came across my old trophies."

"Really?"

"Yeah. I actually put them up when we moved in here. I don't remember if Brian even said anything or not, but I remember putting them all away again one day. They're still packed up. For now. But when I get my own place they're totally going up again!"

"Alicia, this is fantastic! You're honoring the things that make you happy!"

"And next spring I'm going to join a league again. I just decided that right now! Oh, gosh Carrie. I'm going to need to get in shape. Good thing I have some time!"

"Your expression right now is one I haven't seen before. I'd say you look genuinely happy."

Alicia leaned back in her chair and gazed at the monitor for quite a while. "Wow. You're right. I *do* feel happy in a way I haven't in a long time. Which is weird. Nothing's changed since we started talking. I'm still getting divorced. I'm still way worse off financially then I was a few years ago. I still have to get this place ready to sell and find a new place to live…"

"But you changed the most powerful part of your life. You changed your thoughts about your future, and those thoughts made you change your thoughts about your life right now." Carrie reminded her.

"OK, this it totally bizarre, but I just had a flashback to *The Wizard of Oz* when the good fairy says to Dorothy, 'you've always had the power my dear, you just had to learn it for yourself'. This thing about loving softball and looking forward to spring season? That's always been in me. I just needed to … I don't know … remember that it was in me."

"I'm writing that down so I can use it again. I used to love that movie!"

"Me too! And what an amazing movie for its time. To do an entire movie with a female character in the lead who *doesn't* get rescued by a guy or fall in love?!"

"I never thought about that, but you're right! We're definitely watching that for our next family movie night now."

"So, how do I find the other things in my Quality World? I want to get focused on the things that really make me, me."

Carrie grinned. "I'm delighted you asked! You've already experienced the power of shifting your thinking just in our session here today, so it's an easier process because you've bought in."

"Totally," Alicia agreed.

"One thing you can do is frequently ask yourself the question, 'what do I really, *really* want' and write down your answers. Now, not everything you think of right away is actually in your Quality World. It's possible that you'll think of some things that aren't right for you. Maybe things other people have suggested you need, or even things other women are working towards that you just kind of took on as your own goals too without thinking about it.

"The other thing," Carrie continued, "is that you may realize there's things you used to really want that you no longer want, but you've held them in your Quality World anyways."

"I don't get that."

"OK, let me give you an example. When I was younger our family didn't have much money. My mom couldn't work because she was disabled and my dad worked long hours as a mechanic. In my little world, I imagined being a grown up and being able to go to Target every week and buy a cart load of things. That was my idea of success."

"To be fair, that's a pretty common dream."

Carrie nodded. "Then, as an adult, I still had that idea of success but I didn't realize it. I started making money and paying off my debts, and even having savings, but I still felt constantly dissatisfied about money. It was my sister-in-law Jenny that eventually helped. She's a financial planner, and she kept pushing me to define what financial success looked like to me."

She laughed. "In a burst of frustration one day, I actually said that a cart load of stuff at Target was the thing I was missing. That silly comment was my breakthrough."

"So, did you go shopping and exorcise the demon?"

"Kind of the opposite, actually. I wrote a letter to me as a little girl. I honored my dream to have money to buy whatever I wanted. I recognized how hard some things were in my life back then. And then I told myself what true financial success really was and assured that little girl that I would always find a way to provide for myself and the kids."

"OK, Carrie that makes me want to cry!"

"Aw! Before you do, let me wrap it up this way: Writing that letter allowed me to put that picture of shopping for fulfillment into my childhood where it belonged, and place a new picture of financial success in it's place. It totally changed how I see myself and money."

"Is everything we imagined we wanted as children wrong then?"

"Not at all! There's no wrong here, or back then. And *definitely no guilt* for the things we used to want that don't work for us anymore. Whatever decisions and goals we had in the past were done with the best information we had at the time.

"Just because things change, and we change, and our Quality World pictures change, doesn't mean the old things were wrong. Far from it. They were part of the journey. The only important thing is to recognize when those don't work for us anymore and change our pictures to what we truly want right now.

"Wow," Carrie said rubbing her face, "I'm sorry for rambling on there. I get overly passionate about this subject!"

"Hey, no worries! This stuff is so amazing! I'm actually ... I can't believe I'm saying this, but I'm glad Brian isn't with me right now, because I can work through all this, figuring out what I want on my own. I'm still not over the separation and how everything went down. But this part where I'm at right now might be a good thing."

Carrie smiled. "I'm going to be counting the days until we chat again. I can't wait to hear what you learn about yourself and what you want! Oh, one question: you said you wanted to get in shape for soft-ball season. What does that look like?"

"Uh ... I'm not exactly sure. Back then I was always active so I didn't really need to exercise to stay in shape. I'm going to have to get back to you on that. But I promise, in two weeks, I'll have a plan."

"That's fantastic! Have a fun two weeks and we'll chat again soon."

Carrie ended the call with a smile on her face. When she dreamed of being a psychologist she didn't really have a specific idea of what a successful day at work would look like. But the conversation with Alicia—and the whole journey they had been on in the past few months—was exactly what made her feel fulfilled and that she was doing what she was meant to do.

CHAPTER 24

"Hi, Carrie? My name is Dennis and I'm going to be your adoption social worker."

"Hello! Does that mean our application has been approved?"

"It does. Of course, I don't have a match for you yet. I just wanted to call and introduce myself. I expect we'll have some more chats in the future. Bye-bye now."

"Oh, um, bye." Carrie heard the click for the end of the call. She stood at the back door waiting for Maisy to finish doing her business. *Did that really happen?*

"Who was that, Mommy?" Katie asked from kitchen where she was filling up her water bottle. They were getting ready to take Matthew to his friend Liam's, and then they were off to Katie's first gymnastics competition.

"That was a social worker—a new one. His name is Dennis, and he called to say our application is approved but we don't have a match yet."

"I wish Miss Sophie was still our worker. I liked her best!"

"Well, I'm sure Dennis is good, too."

The car ride was spent with Carrie and Jonathan trying to come to terms with their new reality.

"Nothing has really changed," Jonathan said, "even though that call *could* change everything."

"I know. That's the thing. It still feels like we haven't made any real progress. I thought it would feel great not to have that application hanging over our head."

They stopped in front of Liam's house. His little sister Thea was in the front yard, slowly spinning in circles.

Katie rolled down her window and yelled, "Hi Thea!"

Thea stopped for a moment, and flapped one hand in the air before beginning her spinning again.

"So, you'll pick me up around four?" Matthew asked.

"I think so. One of us will text if it's earlier or later than that." Carrie answered.

"K. Bye!" He got out of the car, and carefully opened the front gate to this friend's house and closed it tight behind him. Thea was autistic and would take advantage of anyone who left the front gate unlatched. Carrie watched him say hello to Thea and wait for a response before going to the front door.

Aaron, Liam and Thea's dad, opened the door and let Matthew in before calling to Thea, and waving to Carrie and the rest of the family. Thea shook her head energetically but made her way back inside.

"That man," Jonathan said. "Every time I see him I feel a strange combination of awe and sadness."

"He sure has his work cut out for him," Carrie said quietly.

Later that night, after Katie called all of her grandparents and her

Auntie Jessica to tell them about the participation medal she won at her first competition, Carrie and Jonathan settled onto the loveseat in their bedroom.

"I feel like I'm waiting to get a call about a job," Jonathan said. "You know, when you think you've aced an interview, and you desperately want the job and every time the phone rings you're terrified and hopeful at the same time?"

"That's exactly it! But after we get the 'you've been matched' call, we still have to decide whether to take the job."

He stretched his legs out. "I keep reminding myself what Mark said about them being baby sellers. I want us to make the right decision, but I think the first time I hear about a child I'm going to want to say yes no matter what."

Carrie rested her head on his shoulder. "Walking into the great unknown. Again. Sometimes life can be annoyingly predictable about its unpredictability."

"I'm guessing nothing will happen before Christmas."

"Yeah. Hard to believe it's almost December."

It wasn't even a week later that they got a chance to practice saying no to a child for the first time.

"Carrie? It's Dennis here. Your adoption worker. I'm happy to tell you that you've been matched with a child!"

Carrie had just come upstairs from a morning of counseling sessions to get some lunch. She sat down on the nearest chair, wishing Jonathan wasn't away for work. "Wow, that's great!"

"So, this is a four year old boy. He's healthy, no major issues, and a rather normal pregnancy all things considered. He was placed in an adoptive home a month ago but there's been a breakdown so he's in a temporary foster home. They're overcrowded there, but they've agreed to have him for two weeks."

Carrie felt her heart sink for the little boy who was being shuttled around and was in a place he wasn't truly wanted. She knew that there was a certain time frame before any adoption was final that the parents, the social worker, or even the child if they were old enough could say things weren't working, but it hadn't really seemed like something real. "What happened?"

"I think the adoptive mom just wasn't being realistic. She thought he'd be delighted to be with them and would treat them like his parents right away. When that didn't happen she really struggled to bond with him."

"In a month?" A month wasn't even enough time to get to know a child, let alone decide to give him up!

"Exactly. He does have his challenges, but every kid does. He needs a stable, consistent home where the parents aren't afraid to create a secure environment until he can settle in."

"What do you mean by a secure environment?" Carrie couldn't remember that term being used in the online parenting courses they had taken.

"Well, he's quite the little Houdini. House locks, window locks, car doors, you know."

"Oh, well I guess I need to get ahold of Jonathan. He's traveling for work right now."

"Sure, call me back when you've had a chance to talk to him. This foster home really isn't an ideal placement for him so we'd like to get him into a permanent home as soon as possible."

"OK, I'll get back to you as soon as I can," Carrie said. She hung up the phone and rubbed her eyes. This was not what she had imagined. She pictured trying to weigh the pros and cons, talking to Jonathan and maybe even the kids. But the immediate feeling that this child was not right for them—and the accompanying guilt for feeling so willing to say no to an innocent child—was a dark and heavy disappointment.

She looked at her watch. It was just past three in the morning in Singapore. It would be hours before Jonathan would be awake. She knew he'd call as soon as he was up and she didn't want to get his hopes up by sending a message to call her. She'd just have to wait to talk to him. And in the meantime she still needed to meet with her afternoon clients, take Katie and Matthew shopping for Jonathan's Christmas present like she had promised, and pretend that everything was fine.

Sighing, she got up to make a sandwich for lunch. It was tempting to call one of her friends—or even her mom or sister for that matter—and talk it through, but she couldn't even line up her thoughts in a coherent manner, let alone explain them to someone who wasn't on the same journey she was on.

With her simple lunch made she went in the living room and flicked on the TV, hoping to find something to distract herself with. Instead she ended up flipping through the channels for half an hour while she tried to make herself eat.

Work was a helpful distraction and a good reminder that she wasn't the only one dealing with impossible decisions. By the time she needed to pick up the kids from school to go shopping, a little of the agony she felt during the conversation with Dennis had dulled.

She sat in the student pick up line with the car turned off while she shivered. It was cold enough outside to justify leaving it idling, but she hated the thought of sending more pollution into the air right where little kids would walk by shortly.

Finally she saw Katie running towards her, and she started the car and cranked the heat.

"Hi Mommy! I'm so excited we're going shopping for Daddy's presents! I was thinking about it all day!"

"Hi Katie-girl. Aren't we lucky that we can go shopping like this?"

"Yep!" she said happily while waving to kids out the window. Carrie was pretty sure she didn't know everyone she was waving to, but at least she was friendly! She parked a block away from the high school —Matthew would walk over and meet them as soon as the bell rang. It sure helped to have the staggered start and finish times when she needed to drop off and pick up the kids.

Feeling a little guilty, she kept the car running so Katie wouldn't get cold. When Matthew got in the car he was just as excited as his sister. "There's granola bars and water for snacks," Carrie said as she made her way to the biggest mall in the city.

The Christmas decorations and festive music helped her focus on the fun job of shopping for Jonathan and put the whole adoption business a little more to the back of her mind. It was never totally gone from her thoughts, but it was manageable.

This would be their second Christmas as a proper family. Carrie smiled to herself as she remembered last Christmas. Jonathan had been almost beside himself with excitement, and had made very detailed lists of everything the kids wanted so they could be 'fair' about the gifts they chose.

For Carrie, it had been her first time buying exactly what she wanted for her kids without trying to fit their wish list into an impossibly small budget. They still budgeted, but Jonathan had insisted the amounts were a 'guideline' only.

What had been best about that Christmas was sharing it with Jonathan and feeling like a family. Carrie's parents had also come to their house to stay for a week, making it the first time she hosted her parents for Christmas.

This year they were coming again, and Jessica was flying in on Christmas Eve and staying until the morning of the 27th. The thought that next Christmas might be very different, with another child in their family, got her replaying the phone conversation with Dennis.

"Mom?" Matthew asked as Katie pulled them towards a toy store's display window. "Is something wrong?"

"What? Oh, sorry bud. No, nothing's wrong." She forced a smile on her face. "I guess we should pay attention to whatever catches Katie's eye. Might give us some ideas!"

He gave her a look that said he didn't believe her, and Carrie chastised herself for not hiding her thoughts better. Of course, if Matthew wasn't so tuned in to her moods it would be easier!

By the time they were heading to the food court for dinner, the shopping trip had been declared a success. From Katie, Jonathan would be getting lined Crocs, a t-shirt that said, 'My Daughter Thinks I'm the World's Greatest Dad', and a pack of gourmet chocolates.

He had mentioned that he wanted slippers, but at the department store Katie complained (loudly) that they were all 'Grandpa slippers'. A lady overheard them and recommended lined Crocs instead. Carrie was relieved they met Katie's criteria and they wouldn't have to spend the next two hours looking at the slippers in every single store.

Matthew was getting Jonathan a new leather laptop bag. It was over what Carrie had budgeted, but she knew Jonathan's old one was long past it's expiry date and he'd be proud to tell everyone that it was a gift from his son when he was traveling with it.

"Do you remember the first time we went to a food court?" she asked Matthew once they were sitting down eating.

"I think so. It wasn't this mall, but it was the first time I knew there was more places to eat than McDonald's."

"That was a proud mom moment when I could take you guys there. And now look at us, stopping to eat like we do it all the time."

"We *should* do it all the time, Mommy! I love it here!"

CHAPTER 25

Jonathan agreed with Carrie when they talked the next morning about the 'little Houdini' as Dennis had described him. "I'm totally willing to childproof and make things safe for whatever child comes. Well, if there's anything more we can do beyond everything we did for the homestudy. But a kid that might try to jump out of a moving car? Or one we'd have to lock in his room at night? I can't ... there's no way I could do that."

Carrie breathed a sigh of relief that they were on the same page. "That's really how I felt. Actually, a child like that might even need a home with no other kids—at least to start. I don't know. I'm not an adoption expert or anything so I shouldn't speculate. But what if Dennis doesn't look for more kids for us because we said no to this one?"

"I don't think it works like that but, if that's the way they operate, then it's not the right place for us. I know we said we wanted to help in our own backyard, but I did look into some options for international adoptions yesterday. I guess I just wanted to know what else was out there."

"You mean, from Singapore? I didn't even know there was a chance to do that. It's such a wealthy country."

"Yeah," he let out a half-laugh. "Turns out there's no chance unless we're residents of Singapore. Then I looked at China. I know there used to be tons of orphanages with little girls who had been abandoned. Not much luck there either. Couples in their 'second' marriage need to be married for five years before they can apply."

"Well," Carrie tried to joke, "only three and a half years to go!"

"Riiiight. I guess we just have to have faith that the right child will end up with us at the right time."

"You're right. And I love you so much for being right. And I also love that you'll be on a plane home in less than twelve hours."

"Me too. I can't wait to be back with all of you! Can I talk to the kids?"

"Yep, hang on." Carrie went and opened the bedroom door and called out, "Matthew! Katie! Daddy's on the phone!"

Katie came tearing into the room and grabbed the phone. "Daddy! Daddy! We got your Christmas presents and you're going to looooooooove them!"

Carrie lay down on the bed while Katie talked, and a minute later Matthew joined her. "What are the odds she's going to tell him everything before Christmas?" he said in a low voice.

She turned to look at him. "One hundred percent. Good thing you caught my hint and took her to the dollar store while I paid for your gift to him. One less secret for her to keep."

"Yeah," he said smiling. Then his smiled disappeared. "The school's asking for donations to help needy families over Christmas. It's all for kids that actually go to our school. That has to suck so much to be those kids."

"It's anonymous, right?"

"Well yeah, but still. Can we help out?"

"That's a great idea! Mention it to Jonathan if Katie stops talking long enough to give you a turn, and tell him I'm already on board. It would be good to do something for another family this year."

"Cool."

They ended up going a bit overboard for the families in need, but like Jonathan said, it was something they could actually do for someone else instead of waiting around for their adoption worker to call with another match.

Jonathan and Carrie did all the things families love to do in December—and some they pretended to love to do. They went to a Christmas tree farm to pick out a Christmas tree and took the kids to see Santa Claus. where Matthew acted like he was only doing it for Katie's sake while secretly loving it.

They survived Katie's school's winter concert where they both left with massive headaches and sore backsides from the metal chairs. Matthew's band concert was slightly less painful. They went to a living nativity at their church, and Jonathan took Carrie to hear Handel's *Messiah*. There were Christmas parties at friends' places, girls' lunches out, and guys' nights out.

For Matthew and Katie the season was full of fun, excitement, and anticipation. It had all of those things for Carrie and Jonathan, but they also had a case of the nerves every time the phone rang. They constantly asked themselves 'is my son or daughter out there waiting for me' and sometimes they admitted to each other that they had their doubts that things would work out.

And in the middle of all that, they both continued to work and try and keep their respective clients happy.

Then, on December 23rd, the call came. The kids were both sleeping in and Carrie was in the shower, so Jonathan answered her phone.

"Hi. Oh, Jonathan?"

"Yep. This is Carrie's phone but she's busy right now."

"This is Dennis, your adoption worker."

For the first time, Jonathan got to experience the immediate heart-pounding that Carrie had described. "Oh, hi Dennis," he said, trying to keep his voice level.

"So, I've got a potential match I'd like you and Carrie to consider."

"OK…"

"Now, I know you indicated you were looking for a single child, but a sibling group has just come onto our office's case load and I think they might be a good fit for you."

Jonathan tried to say something, but nothing came out.

"It's two children," Dennis continued, "a boy and a girl. She's three and he's one. They were taken into care almost a year ago, and they've been living with an uncle and aunt who were hoping to adopt them, but the couple is getting on in years. So, they're really not in a position to care for little ones but they'd like to remain in the children's lives."

"Well, uh…" Jonathan tried to remember the questions he and Carrie had agreed to ask but his mind was blank.

"Now, we wouldn't do anything over Christmas, but I wanted to give you a chance to consider a sibling group. I know it's a big decision, but from what I've read from your application, you and your wife are more than able to give these two a great home."

"Is there, um, is there anything else we should know about them?" He knew that was a much more vague question than what Carrie would have asked, but at least he got something out!

"Well, their file says that they are a bit developmentally delayed but they're catching up. I think there's someone helping with that, and of course that help would continue after they're placed."

"Oh, OK."

"So go have a wonderful Christmas and just keep these two kids in mind. I'll give you a call before the new year and we can talk more."

"Sure, thank you."

"Ok. Bye-bye now."

Jonathan leaned forward in his chair. It felt like he couldn't quite take a deep breath. Ten minutes later that's where Carrie found him.

"Are you OK?"

"I don't think so. That was Dennis. He's asked us to consider taking two kids. Siblings. Three and one. Um, darn it. I would have written down what he said if I was thinking. Something about they're with an uncle and aunt who wanted to adopt them, but they're old so they can't. But I think he said they want to stay in contact."

Carrie knelt down on the floor beside him. "Well, now I know why you looked like you were having trouble breathing. We never even talked about more than one child. Actually, we said no to that on the application."

"I know. I'm ... well, still having trouble with words here. I couldn't think of the questions to ask that we had agreed on. All I asked was if there were any problems or something. He said there were delays, but they had a team in place that would stay with the kids. Whatever that means."

"Hmmm, developmental delays aren't the end of the world if they're temporary. Like, if they're due to environment, the kids can catch up and generally do. Or if they were born prematurely, those kids often catch up with the right support. Did he say if there was any prenatal exposure?"

Jonathan snapped a finger. "*That's* one of the questions. Seriously Carrie. I need those written down if we get any more calls like that one. It's like getting hit by an invisible train."

"So he didn't say anything."

"I don't think so. What would be a reason for those delays where the kids wouldn't catch up?"

"Well, brain damage for one. Like if they didn't get oxygen during the delivery. I can't remember what else but there must be other things. Of course, alcohol exposure."

"Can they tell which kids have fetal alcohol syndrome when they're born?"

Carrie pulled out her phone. "Only if it's severe, or if birth mom was binge drinking when facial features were developing. Here, these images help. The babies can have smaller eye openings, and the nose ridge between their eyes can be flatter. Plus a shorter nose, a thin upper lip, and right here below their nose is smooth. Some other things, too, I'm sure. The thing is, it's different for every child. And a lot of the delays will show up over time when they miss milestones."

Jonathan touched the phone. "I would fall in love with any one of these kids."

"You're a good man Jonathan Brandt."

Carrie didn't have any trouble waking up early on Christmas morning. Between the excitement of her sister and parents coming and thoughts about the two children Dennis had called about, she was struggling to fall asleep and stay asleep. It was easier to get up and do something so she quietly put her robe on and went downstairs.

She brewed herself a cup of coffee from the fancy machine Jonathan had given her as an anniversary gift, and turned on the oven to preheat for the overnight cinnamon buns she'd made the night before.

They hadn't told anyone about the call. It was too vague and uncertain to share with the kids so they decided to just keep it to themselves entirely. In some ways it made it easier because Carrie knew it would've been their sole topic of conversation. But she felt lost and confused and hopeful all at the same time and it would've been nice to share that burden with her family.

When Katie woke up, the house woke up, and Carrie did her best to lose herself in the magic and the busyness of the day.

In the afternoon, Max, Jenny, Angela, Brielle, and Jenny's parents all came over for Christmas dinner. Her parents were enjoying an extended stay to help out with baby Brielle.

Just as Carrie had predicted, Angela had not only stopped watching toddler shows, but took her job as a big sister seriously. She could already change a diaper and even feed Brielle with a little supervision. Jenny was delighted in the changes, but also struggling with seeing her little girl grow up.

The sisters-in-law were setting the table while Jessica took Angela, Katie, and Maisy for a walk. Carrie's mom and Jenny's mom were visiting in the living room, and the guys were in the garage looking at Jonathan's car.

Jenny moved the big Christmas centerpiece to the sideboard to make more room on the table. "I've started asking Angela to bring her story books over when I'm feeding Brielle. I tell her it's good for Brielle to hear us reading out loud but it's really because it's the best way to still get cuddles from Angela!"

"You're doing so good with them," Carrie said. "And I'm glad to see Max has recovered so nicely from labor and delivery."

The three of them used any chance to tease him about the day his daughter was born. Max took it in stride, and had admitted soon after that he couldn't explain what had come over him. Carrie encouraged him to go for some counseling and he was starting with her mentor in the new year.

"I think it's really going to help him," Jenny admitted. "He tends to keep his worries bottled up. I guess the result of that is they explode during the worst time."

"You can say that again! I'm really glad he's going. With Dr. Henshaw's approach he'll probably only need a few sessions to get this off his chest and learn some new strategies for processing his worries."

It seemed like everyone came back into the house at once, and soon the kitchen was overflowing with people putting finishing touches on their signature dishes while the smell of turkey had the kids and Maisy hovering close by, waiting for the invitation to dinner.

After Jonathan said grace, Carrie's dad stood up and looked at the table loaded with tantalizing, festive dishes. "I'd like to take a quick minute to toast Carrie and Jonathan. It's pretty clear you've created a warm, welcoming home. Coming here always feels like a vacation for Julia and I. So we've decided to make it permanent. In the New Year we'll be house shopping!" He raised his glass. "To Carrie and Jonathan, Jessica, Max and Jenny, and Tom and Martha, and to these wonderful kids Matthew, Katie, Angela, Brielle, and the children yet to join us. Cheers!"

They all toasted and exclaimed over the unexpected news. Katie had to nearly yell to be heard above the conversation. "Grandpa!"

He paused with a bowl of mashed potatoes in his hand. "Yes?"

"You forgot someone!"

Looking around the table he said, "Oh no! Who did I forget?"

"Maisy!"

They all chuckled as he added a quick toast to Maisy.

Jessica was sitting beside Carrie, "Bit of a far cry from our four-person Christmas dinners as kids, hey?"

Carrie nodded, "And I didn't even know about all this stuff we were missing when we cooked turkey dinner! Sweet potatoes with marshmallows on top? Brussel sprouts sautéed with pancetta? Orange and honey glazed carrots?"

"I know right?" Jessica said with her mouth full. After swallowing she continued, "these rosemary dinner rolls are to die for. If I was working here, I'd make turkey sandwiches and eat them at my desk to make all the non-gluten people drool."

"You do know that some of those people actually can't have gluten, right?

"Not the ones in my office! They run after the next fad like it's life or death. And then all they talk about is how much they miss whatever food they're not eating."

"Well, I have to say I'm ridiculously grateful today that I *can* eat everything here. So, what do you think of Mom and Dad's announcement?" Carrie asked.

"I did think they'd make the move, but I thought it wouldn't be for another year or so. Do you think they can afford it? I know they want to downsize, but things in the city are a lot more expensive."

"I don't even know if there are any accessible places for sale," Carrie added. "They'll probably have to find something they can renovate."

Jessica was interrupted by Tom asking a question about a neighbor who'd been injured at work. While they talked, Carrie basked in the sights and sounds of a happy holiday dinner.

Her thoughts wandered to the two children who were waiting for their forever home. They *were* living with family, which should make their Christmas better. And being so young they probably didn't know that big changes were planned for their future.

What were the uncle and aunt thinking? Were they trying to take in all the memories of their last Christmas with the kids? She hoped the couple would be supported as they started on this changing journey.

"Remember to eat," Jonathan said quietly.

"Oh, right. I was getting lost in thought."

"I know. It's hard to stay present right now. Well," he paused as he reached for more turkey, "maybe not *that* hard. Everything here is amazing! I sure hope my parents can see this." He looked at Max. "And I hope they can see how happy Max and I are. I never dreamed life could be this good."

"Yeah. It's quite something to go from hoping I can collect enough soda cans to cover groceries to being married, and in this big gorgeous house, surrounded by happy, healthy extended family."

"Lots to be grateful for," he said, holding up his wineglass.

Carrie clinked her own glass to his. "Definitely lots to be grateful for."

"Cheers Mommy!" Katie said from across the table. Carrie reached across and clinked her glass to Katie's, and then to Angela's who was sitting beside her. Further down the table she could see Matthew having a deep discussion with his grandpa and his honorary grandpa.

She felt something warm and soft brush against her leg and she looked under the table. "Maisy! Back to your mat silly girl!" With a wagging tail Maisy crawled out from under the table and went back to the mat where she stayed (or was supposed to stay) during mealtimes. They were going to need to buy her a bigger mat soon. And a bigger bed, for that matter. Maisy had already outgrown the predictions from the shelter and didn't seem to be slowing down.

And I don't even have to worry about affording dog food Carrie thought with a smile.

CHAPTER 27

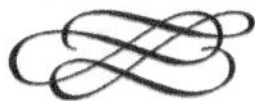

"Hi Carrie, this is Dennis. How was your Christmas?"

"Hi Dennis. It was great! We're enjoying having my parents for an extended stay while the kids are on holidays."

"Good. Good. Listen, have you and Jonathan given any thought to the sibling group?"

Any thought? Carrie almost rolled her eyes. *Try every thought!* "Uh, we're a little nervous about the idea, but interested."

"OK great! I'd like to plan an info sharing session. That's where we'll meet in person with the children's social worker and she'll give you more detailed information about the kids and answer any questions you have."

"That sounds like a good idea."

"I already have some dates the other social worker is available. How about the first Wednesday of the New Year? I think the kids are back to school on the Tuesday…"

"Wednesday I'm at the clinic. We could do Thursday or Friday though. Actually, Friday would be better so I don't have to cancel any clients."

They agreed on Friday morning. Carrie looked at the calendar. Nine sleeps away. Well, they'd just have to make it through. She debated sharing with their friends. Of course, if this was the right match they could all celebrate. But if it wasn't right, they'd all struggle to process it. And there was still a part of her that felt like she was 'child shopping'. It was necessary and wrong all at the same time.

By the time Friday arrived, she and Jonathan agreed that it was too hard to take this journey alone. Regardless of the outcome of their morning info sharing, they'd include their closest friends and family in the journey going forward.

Things started off on a positive note. They sat in comfortable chairs around a low table and the children's social worker was personable and positive.

"It's a really difficult time for the uncle and aunt, of course, but they're confident they're doing the right thing for the children. There was some talk before placement about their age—they're both in their sixties—but these days parents and grandparents of all ages are raising kids, aren't they?"

Carrie already felt admiration for the couple who had taken in these two children at a time when most couples were beginning to enjoy their retirement.

"So," the social worker continued, "Sarah and Evan are already in some early intervention programs. A few of the programs are in-home where the therapists come to your home, and a few of them are in-office and you'll need to be able to drive them there. We can help out with the costs of transportation, and we'll continue to cover the costs of their therapies."

Carrie and Jonathan exchanged looks. This was new. They had assumed that any costs related to the children would be their responsibility.

"How many days a week do they have therapy?" Jonathan asked.

"Five days a week for Sarah and three days a week for Evan. They're fantastic programs and it's really exciting to see their progression. Plus they're very sweet kids and all the therapists love them."

The social worker continued talking as Dennis, Jonathan, and Carrie listened. She talked about the children's siblings, some of whom live with the birth mom or birth dad, and how they may want contact in the future. She described the playset the uncle had built and how the aunt loved to knit.

"And I have some pictures of the kids!" she added excitedly. "Of course, I can't let you take them home today, but once they're placed with you I have a whole box of pictures right back to when they were babies.

They leaned forward to look at the pictures the social worker was laying on the table. Carrie heard Dennis take a deep breath in. She picked up two of the pictures so she and Jonathan could have a closer look. Her stomach started to hurt and her heart sank.

The meeting wrapped up with the children's social worker still chatting about how far the kids had come with their therapy and how wonderful the uncle and aunt were. Dennis followed Carrie and Jonathan to the elevator.

As soon as the doors closed, Carrie turned to Dennis, "What's going on here?" she asked, her voice shaky. "First you ask us to consider a sibling group even though we didn't agree to one in our application. And then you get our hopes up and bring us here for two children with severe Fetal Alcohol Syndrome requiring full-time intervention?"

Dennis ran his hands through his thinning hair. "Guys, I'm so sorry. I had no idea. It's the first time I've seen pictures too. This is not ... I should have checked more carefully before agreeing to this match. I apologize."

"Hey, you've got an incredibly hard job here," Jonathan said. "It's a job I could never do, and I respect that. But it's been hard enough for us to come to grips with what we can handle, and how to grow our family without doing long-term harm to Matthew and Katie. There's ... you know, it's hard to even say out loud, but there's no way we could take those kids and still be available to parent the kids we already have."

Dennis nodded. "You're absolutely right." He gave a half smile. "You'll hear from me again, but I promise I'll have all the information about the child before I even call you."

The elevator dinged and the door opened. Carrie gave a little wave goodbye while Jonathan shook Dennis' hand.

When they were in the car she doubled over, "I feel sick. How could she do that?"

"Honestly? I think she truly loves those kids and believes they're going to be fine."

"But they ... ugh. I can't."

Jonathan put his hand on her shoulder. "Then don't. Don't try to process it, or understand it, or anything. Just let it go. Whatever's right for us will happen when it happens. We have so much to be thankful for. Let's focus on that."

Carrie nodded and sat up slowly. She leaned back and closed her eyes while Jonathan drove them home.

"I'm so glad we didn't tell anyone about this one," she admitted when they were home.

"Me too. But I still think we shouldn't go through any more of this alone. Deal?"

"Deal."

CHAPTER 28

Carrie woke up the next morning feeling tired and discouraged. Normally the weekend was her favorite time, when they did things as a family and had a more relaxed schedule. But today she couldn't get excited about anything.

"Hi Mommy!" Katie said as she came downstairs in her nightie. She crawled onto the couch where Carrie was sitting drinking a coffee and cuddled in. "What are we doing today?"

She kissed the top of Katie's head. "I think we're just going to have a lazy morning at home."

"Aw, that's not fun. Can't we do something? Please?"

"See what Daddy says when he comes down."

"OK! Can I watch TV?"

"Sure." Carrie scrolled absentmindedly through her phone while Katie zone out to whatever was on TV. Maisy sat at their feet, occasionally lifting her head if she thought they were going to get up. Carrie knew the dog could use a walk, but she just didn't have it in her.

Matthew and Jonathan came down at the same time, trying to decide on breakfast. Eventually they agreed on French toast and sausages. The hum of conversation as they cooked together was soothing.

During breakfast Katie threw out ideas of what they could do until Jonathan agreed to take them skating. "We'll see if Angela and Magnus and his brothers want to come too."

Magnus was Kara's youngest son. His twin brothers were now fifteen years old and passionate about rugby, which was supposed to use up some of their energy. It never seemed to work. A few years ago, Carrie had babysat the three boys after school every day. Just the thought of having them all over now without their parents to run interference was overwhelming.

"I hope just Magnus can come," Katie said.

Carrie forced herself to take Maisy for a walk with Katie while the guys were cleaning up breakfast, but as soon as Maisy had done her business they turned around and came back home.

"Can't we stop at the playground Mommy? I think Maisy wants to watch me on the swings!"

"Not today Katie-girl."

She decided to stay home when everyone else went skating. There were two orders for frames and paintings that needed packing up, but there wouldn't be parcel pick up until Monday morning and she figured there was no rush getting it done early.

Saturday afternoon TV left a lot to be desired, and she ended up flipping through Netflix without managing to choose anything to watch until everyone was home again.

"Do you want to go out to the movies tonight?" Jonathan asked.

"Not really. I'm kind of tired, I think I need to go to bed early."

He gave her a worried look but didn't say anything.

For the next few weeks, Carrie did the bare minimum to get by. Her online counseling sessions were full of happy clients who spent the entire hour talking about how things were working out. Alicia had taken up kick-boxing to get in shape, and she couldn't stop talking about how great she felt, and how her break-up from Brian had been so good for her.

One of Alicia's referrals from her IVF support group was now three months pregnant, and she really did seem to glow as she talked to Carrie about the relief of passing the three month mark, and how fantastic she was feeling now that the morning sickness had passed.

Another of the referrals was over the moon because a distant cousin had decided she couldn't raise a baby after all, and things were proceeding for her and her husband to adopt the baby.

Everyone was happy and fulfilled, but Carrie felt stuck in a rut she couldn't get out of. When she made it to her basement studio, she found the frames all looked the same and she didn't have any fresh ideas. A potential commission fell through because the client didn't get the office space he was hoping for, and all Carrie felt was relief that she wouldn't have a big job hanging over her head.

"How can I help you?" Jonathan finally asked one night as they sat on their loveseat.

"What do you mean?"

"You've become so quiet the last two weeks. Ever since the meeting with the adoption worker. And even though you're going to bed earlier and earlier, you're a lot more tired than usual. Plus, you just seem sad. I wish I could make things better for you. Is there anything I can do to help?"

Carrie was surprised when her eyes filled with tears. It was the first real emotion she had felt in a while. "I guess I am sad," she whispered, "but I have no reason to be."

"Are you depressed?"

She shrugged. "I don't really know what that means for me. Maybe.

I, I don't know. Maybe I need to be blah for a while. I mean, the past seven or eight years I've felt constant pressure to survive, and then to provide for the kids, and then to finish school, and build the frame business and the counseling business…"

"And then you had to go and collect yourself a needy husband," Jonathan's eyes dimmed.

Carrie turned her body and snuggled against his strong chest. "You've met more of my needs than I could have ever imagined."

"Except the need for more kids."

She sat up and stared at him, "What on earth? No way. We don't know why we didn't get pregnant and now you're totally supporting the adoption process."

"Are you sure Carrie? Are you sure it's not me? Maybe deep down you're unhappy that you're not pregnant and you're questioning your decision."

"What decision?"

"The decision to marry me."

Tears started to fall down Carrie's cheeks, and Jonathan dropped his head into his hands. "No, Jonathan. I'm not crying because you're right. I'm crying because I'm devastated that you'd ever think I'd regret marrying you. I may be down in the dumps right now but there's nothing from you that makes me feel that way. Nothing."

He raised his head slowly, tears in his own eyes, "Are you sure? Completely sure?"

She cupped his cheeks in her hands and wiped away his tears with her thumbs. "Yes, completely sure. One hundred percent of every second of every minute of every day I know that marrying you was the best decision I ever made."

"Phew!" He sank back against the loveseat, trying—unsuccessfully

—to let out a laugh. "I just thought, since you've never been like this, that it had to be because of me."

The next morning Carrie made an appointment with Dr. Henshaw. She kept seeing the look on Jonathan's face when he asked if she regretted marrying him. Whatever her problem was, she needed to figure it out so she didn't hurt him like that again.

"Carrie!" Dr. Henshaw said as he opened his office door. "Welcome!"

"Thanks. Wow, I've never seen your private office before. It's beautiful."

He chuckled. "Well, there's the people I see at the clinic who have a certain expectation. And then there's the people who see me here who have a different expectation. I think about you and your online practice every month when I write my rent check for this office. And then I remember that computer screens give me terrible headaches."

She sat down in an armchair and he sat across from her.

"So, tell me what's been going on."

Taking a deep breath, she began to explain her history and kept talking until she had covered her talk with Jonathan where he thought he was her problem. "I don't really know what's going on with me, but when it starts to impact my family it's time to figure something out."

"Have you taken any time to heal?"

"You mean from Don?"

"From anything that's hurt you."

"Well, for a while when I was still single I was getting these terrible nightmares about Don coming and taking the kids from me. It got to the point where I wasn't getting a full night's sleep ever. So I started writing about it. I'd start with a part of the nightmare that I remembered, and then I'd rewrite the ending. At first it always ended with something bad happening to Don, but then it kind of progressed to silliness. And I'd always give myself a happy ending. After a while, the nightmares slowed and then stopped."

She smiled. "And of course, marrying Jonathan has really mended my heart. He thinks the world of the kids and I, and he's proud of me and super supportive. It's still, I don't know, strange, I guess to be in a completely equal marriage. But I am getting used to it!"

"OK. So, you've told me your background. And you've told me about the things you've done to change your life for the better. Perhaps now you could tell me what you want next. What's in your future?"

"Well, that's the thing. I don't know. This last adoption fiasco really sent me for a loop. I thought I was going to be physically sick when I realized that the social worker was being so dishonest—whether it was intentional or not."

"You wanted a different behavior from her."

"Yes!"

"So, she gave you information about her agenda and what she was willing to do. Information, I might add, that is entirely her choice to give or not give. And you took that information personally because you couldn't control her or make her tell you the truth."

"Ouch."

"Oh, it's not meant to be hurtful. I'm looking at your response and the purpose behind it. You know that with everything we say and do we have a goal."

Carrie sighed. "Yes, I know that. And I suppose it was about trying to control her. More than that it's about trying to control an outcome that's out of my control. If we would have gotten pregnant, I would've been in control. You know, with a specific due date, and maybe even a gender. I know what to expect with a newborn so I would have prepared for that. Adoption is so ... uncontrollable. And open-ended. I don't know if that explains how down I've been feeling but it definitely explains my reaction to that meeting."

"We've known each other for over a year now. And I respect you, both as a person and as a counselor. So please know that I wouldn't say this to just anyone. Carrie, is it possible that a part of you has *chosen* to depress because you want to have something in your life you can completely control? I know your background in Choice Theory makes it theoretically possible to acknowledge the choice to depress, but have you considered that you're this as part of your own coping strategy?"

Carrie bit back her first instinct, which was to retort that *of course* she hadn't chosen to depress. Her second thought was to begrudgingly acknowledge that he may be right. From the outside, nobody would know how important control was to her. But the reason she had always been so driven—at least part of the reason—was because she was the only thing she could control in a very out-of-control world.

"I really don't want to admit it, but you may be right." She let out a sigh. This is exactly what she challenged her own clients to do. Face their responsibility to choose what they thought, said, and did. And she knew that making new choices would change things. But she was also aware of a small part of her that just wanted to keep doing what she was doing. And then she remember the look in Jonathan's eyes when he asked if he was the problem. "OK. What do I do?"

"Start by tuning in to your thoughts. What are you thinking about throughout your day? Positive and true thoughts? Negative thoughts? Stressed out imaginations about how things might go wrong? All of those thoughts will impact how you feel.

"When you do feel down, you can either try to backtrack to identify what thought triggered the decision to depress and consciously change that thought, or you can decide that you won't let yourself depress and work on fresh and helpful thoughts. Two different processes, similar results."

He paused and leaned forward. "I will add an important caveat. If the decision to stop depressing becomes overwhelming, or you find yourself losing a battle with dark thoughts, it's time for an external intervention. If that happens you either call me, or if I'm not available you get yourself to the hospital. Agreed?"

"For sure," she responded. "I don't think it will go that direction, though. I *can* work through this. In a way it's the same thing as the nightmares. I need to rewrite my story from this point forward and change the ending. The more I do that, the better I'll feel."

"Yes! That's exactly it! And thank you for not throwing your chair at me a few minutes ago. You looked tempted."

Carrie laughed and was surprised that it felt natural, "I may have been tempted, but only for a second. Thank you so much Dr. Henshaw."

"You're very welcome. Please call or come back in any time."

"Are you happy now Mommy?" Katie asked while eating breakfast a few mornings later.

"Well, I *am* feeling better. But sometimes we feel sad for a while. And that's OK."

Katie's face twisted and she seemed to be trying to figure something out. "I'm not sad. Well, Maisy made me sad yesterday when she pulled at the leash and made me fall and hurt my knee. But then she came and licked my face." She giggled. "That made me happy and the sad was all gone!"

"You're made in a very special way Katie. A way that helps you see the happy things everywhere, and a way that the sad things don't make you sad for very long. But other people aren't that way. They're going to be sad. Sometimes for a long time. And they can't always do something about it."

"That's not fair! Everyone should be made to be happy!"

Jonathan walked in the room and kissed Katie on the forehead and Carrie on the lips. "Morning ladies. Are we enjoying life lessons with Katie?"

"Daddy, were you ever really sad for a long time?"

Jonathan made a cup of coffee and joined them at the table. "Yes. Once, a long time ago I loved someone very much and then she died in a car accident. That made me very sad for a long time. And then my mom and dad died in a car accident. And I was still sad about that when I met you."

"But you're not sad now, right?"

"Well, I have a lot more happy times—lots of them are thanks to you because you make me happy. But sometimes I'm still very sad that my mom and dad aren't here. I miss them."

"It's stupid that people die in car crashes."

"I agree."

Carrie drank the last of her coffee and stood up. "Finish up your breakfast. You need time to put your snow pants on today for walking to school. It's cold outside!"

Jonathan groaned. "Do we have to walk today?"

"*You* don't have to do anything. But *I'm* walking Katie to school this morning. I need the exercise and fresh air. Plus, Maisy needs practice heeling when there are more kids around."

He sighed. "You're right. And what time did Matthew leave the house?"

"I just caught him on his way out the door at 7:15. He must really love band to be willing to get himself out the door so early."

"I'm not doing band when I'm in high school." Katie said as she drank the last of the milk out of her cereal bowl. "Nurses don't need to know band."

"OK, clean up and go brush your teeth," Carrie answered.

When she was out of earshot, Jonathan grinned. "I'll bet she'll join band if her friends do."

"No doubt. So, are you staying here?"

"No, I'll walk with you. But for the record, I'm a big fan of driving kids to school."

"Noted," Carrie answered as she rolled her eyes.

"Did you just roll your eyes at me?"

"Yep!"

Ten minutes later they were bundled up and walking to school. Maisy was still growing and seemed to be forgetting some of her training at the same time. She was over 70 pounds, and her head was almost at Carrie's waist. The dog trainer said it was like she was a teenager now, and they needed to be firm and consistent. He also warned them that she would probably continue to grow for the next two years. They joked that her mom was a stray and her dad was a bear.

When they got closer to the school Jonathan insisted on taking the leash. "I can do it!" Katie insisted, but then looked grateful when Jonathan had to use two hands to keep Maisy at a heel when kids started to call her name. She was already a bit of a celebrity at the school yard.

They said goodbye to Katie, who ran off to play with her friends until the bell rang, and stayed put while kids came over to say hi to the dog. Once Jonathan got Maisy into a sit she was perfectly behaved, and allowed the kids to crowd around her while her tail wagged non-stop.

Carrie preferred to stand a foot or so back and watch the kids as they interacted with the big dog. She hoped to be able to bring Maisy into schools and maybe even care homes eventually, but the trainer had told her they needed to wait until they were confident she was under control at all times. "She's so big she could accidentally hurt someone and that would be the end of her public life."

On the way back home Carrie held the leash and Maisy walked at a perfect heel. "She really is like a teenager. Lovely and perfectly behaved one minute, and crazy the next!"

"Yeah. I want to spend some time with just Matthew to make sure he can handle her when he walks her. I couldn't believe how strong she was back there when she wanted to get to the kids."

"At least she likes kids."

"Likes them?" Jonathan reached down to pet the dog. "She lives for them. We're just her substitute kids until the real ones come in the door after school."

"Maybe we should get some daytime kids for her," Carrie joked. It was nice to be able to joke again. She still experienced some moments in the day where she felt the negative thoughts try to take over, but they seemed less. Feeling like joking and teasing again was a good sign that maybe the worst was behind her—or at least she was better prepared for big disappointments.

Back home she changed from warm walking clothes to warm business clothes for her day at the clinic. "You've got your phone on?" she asked Jonathan as she slipped into her favorite boots.

"On, charged, with the ringer turned up. Like I do every Wednesday so you can keep yours off."

She reached up and kissed him. "Sorry. And thank you."

"Have a good day!"

"You too! And you be good Maisy," she said, stopping to give Maisy a little pet before leaving. Even though she was a handful, Carrie couldn't imagine not having the dog. She had become an important part of their family.

As she drove to work she repeated the mantra that had gotten her through many difficult times. Alone in the car she said 'I love myself' over and over to the beat of the soft jazz she liked to listen to when she wanted to relax.

The clinic was bustling as usual and Carrie didn't get a chance to see Kara until after her first client. Then they briefly passed in the hall, agreeing to try and take lunch at the same time so they could visit. Carrie's schedule was a lot more predictable than Kara's who often just grabbed bites of food between patients so she wouldn't run too far behind. As a physician's assistant she was often the first choice for anyone who might not need a doctor for treatment.

At noon after Carrie's last morning client left, she stayed in the office to type up her notes before going for lunch. It was the best way to avoid spending an hour at the clinic after it closed trying to catch up on paperwork. But her office door suddenly swung open, startling her.

"Carrie!" Kara said breathlessly. "It's Jonathan on the phone! Line 3!"

Knowing he wouldn't call unless it was an emergency she quickly grabbed the phone as Kara took a seat in one of the armchairs.

"Hey!"

"Carrie! I just got a call from Dennis—"

"Oh thank goodness. I thought something bad had happened to one of the kids!" She gave a thumbs up to Kara, who looked relieved.

"No, nothing bad. But maybe something good! Really good! We've been matched with two kids! They're a boy and a girl. She's five and he's one. Um, let me see, I tried to write it all down. Birth mom says she did some cocaine when she was pregnant with the boy, nothing with the girl. They've been with the same foster family since they were apprehended seven months ago, and the guardianship order just went through!"

Carrie leaned back in her chair and closed her eyes. Her first thought was *No, not this again.* But Jonathan sounded so excited. "Wow. This is really ... unexpected."

"But it's perfect, right? I mean, you and I would have to cut back on some work with two kids at home. Oh yeah, he said the five year old isn't in school yet. But we could totally do this!" It sounded like his mind was already made up.

"Whoa. Remember last time? This sounds great right now, but we don't have the whole story. And I think we need to try not get too excited yet. There's lots that could go wrong, or that we could find out that wouldn't work for us."

"I know. You're right. But something about it just *feels* right this time Carrie! I think this is it! Of course I told Dennis I'd talk to you first before anything else. You're OK if I call him back and tell him to tell their social worker that we're interested, right?"

She wanted to scream 'no'. She had just gotten over the last heart-breaking match and she really didn't want to go through it again. "Do you want to take a day or two and think about it?"

"Are you kidding? There's no way I could sleep!"

"Well, I guess it doesn't hurt to say we're interested …"

"Yes! You're awesome! I'll call him right away! Bye! I love you!"

The phone clicked and Carrie slowly put the handset down.

"Well, the sound of Jonathan's voice coming through the phone sure doesn't match your face. What's up?" Kara asked.

"Are you free for lunch?"

"Yep, all caught up and my next patient isn't until one."

"Let's get lunch and I'll tell you all about it." At least she and Jonathan had agreed it was OK to share their journey with friends and family this time around. Carrie felt like she was going to need all the support she could get.

By the time they got to their favorite café a block away, Carrie had told Kara everything she knew about the potential match.

"I don't understand. Why aren't you jumping up and down for joy?"

"Besides the fact that I might wipe out on the slippery sidewalk?"

Carrie joked. "Because the last time we went through this it turned out to be nothing like we had been told and I was devastated. I kind of spiraled down and was miserable for weeks. I've just started to feel like myself again."

They stopped at the till to order and pay before sitting down. The café was a favorite for many of the medical offices in the area, and everyone paid for their meals right away in case they needed to suddenly leave.

Kara took a long drink of her Coke. "Ah, the magic of caffeine and sugar," she said with a smile. "Since we're short on time I'm going to pass right by the part where you were going through some major life stuff and didn't include me. But I promise you, you'll hear from me about that!" She paused for another drink. "So tell me Carrie, why do you think this match will turn out exactly like the last one?"

"Dang it Kara. Cut right to the chase why don't you?"

"I always do," Kara said with a smile.

"Yeah. I usually love that about you but today I'd like to wallow in self-pity and be miserable for a bit before admitting that there's no basis for the way I feel and I'm just being negative because I want to."

"Looks like I'm not the only one willing to cut to the chase! Listen, last time you guys did this alone. Which I do *not* approve of. This time you've got your people around you. Whether it works out or not, we've got you. And it's going to be OK."

CHAPTER 30

"Are you ready for this?" Jonathan asked as he held open the door to the social work offices.

"Honestly? No, I'm not. I want to go home and pretend this isn't happening."

He took her hand gently as they waited for the elevator. "You know what? We've got everything. Two wonderful kids, a great dog, a home we love, good jobs, good friends." The elevator doors opened and they walked in. "If this does work out, it's a bonus. *Not* life and death. If it doesn't work out, we're not actually losing anything."

Carrie tried to smile for her husband. "You're right. Except you forgot to say that we have each other."

He leaned forward and kissed her. "That's the most important one."

After sitting in the waiting room for almost twenty minutes, Dennis rushed in from the elevator. "Sorry guys, had some things come up that needed dealing with. Just give me a sec to see if Wendy's here and then I'll come back and get you."

Jonathan squeezed Carrie's hand.

"Yep, we're good to go. Again, sorry to keep you waiting. Right this way." He led them into a conference room where a lady with greying hair wearing a dark green suit was already sitting down.

She stood up when they came in. "Hello! I'm Wendy. I'm Abigail and Logan's social worker."

Carrie wanted to be neutral and reserved about the meeting, but she found herself immediately liking Wendy. Although she seemed more like a grandma than a social worker.

"So, I've read your entire adoption application, and Dennis has updated me on your previous experience with matching. First I'd like to say that you are my first choice for these children, but you are not my only choice. This must be right for you. If it's not, I assure you that these children will still end up in a good forever home."

Carrie found herself relaxing and Jonathan put an arm around her. *Like night and day between this social worker and the last one!* she thought to herself.

"Second," Wendy continued, "I've been doing this job for a long time and I'm very good at it. I understand the full cycle of adoption, and what a placement like this means to a family. As you'll hear, these children are different than most of the children in the system, but they will still bring challenges. I will do my best to clearly communicate those so you can make an educated decision about what's best for you."

Dennis leaned forward. "She's the rock star of her entire department. Every time she tries to retire they find a way to trap her in for another year."

Wendy waved a dismissing hand at him. "Don't mind him. He's just intimidated because I'm older than his mother. Now. Let's talk about Abigail and Logan. Actually, I'll start with birth mom. She had some struggles with drugs and alcohol in high school, and dropped out in eleventh grade when she got pregnant. She claims she didn't drink, smoke, or do drugs during her pregnancy and after Abigail was born, her parents watched the baby during the day so she could finish high school. At the time she hoped to become an interior decorator."

After a pause to take a sip from her water bottle, Wendy continued. "Birth mom did graduate, but then she reconnected with Abigail's birth dad and things went wrong from there. She moved out of her parent's home when Abigail was two, and in with him. At some point she became addicted to cocaine.

"When she got pregnant again, she claims she stopped doing drugs. However, Logan was born with cocaine in his system and remained in hospital for ten days to go through withdrawal treatment. It does seem like the withdrawal wasn't too bad, which could indicate less exposure. By the time he was discharged, birth mom claimed she had kicked birth dad out and was committed to raising her children.

"Social services did follow up, and initial reports suggested that she was keeping a clean, safe home and doing well, under the circumstances. After a month, they closed the file. Then a few weeks later a neighbor called the police to report two children left in the hallway of the apartment building where they lived.

"Four-year-old Abigail was holding a very quiet baby Logan when the police arrived. They immediately transported the children to the hospital where it was determined that they were both suffering from mild malnutrition and Logan had a sinus infection and severe diaper rash.

"The police had to break down the apartment door to take birth mom into custody, and found five people in the apartment all high. When birth mom was sober a day later and learned what had happened to her children, she apparently begged the social worker to take her parental rights away and never let her near the children again."

Carrie found herself unwillingly placing herself in birth mom's shoes. What had she been feeling? To be dealing with the all-consuming power of addiction and then to find out that you had nearly killed your own children? She couldn't imagine the weight of that realization.

"This isn't the way these types of things usually play out," Wendy said. "It's much more likely that the birth parent will make excuses, get a lawyer, and insist their children be placed back with them. Of course, it's always our first aim to help birth parents recover and keep families together, but in this case the mom only agreed to one final meeting to say good-bye to the children. The report says she cried through the entire meeting and begged the children and the social worker to forgive her."

"Where's the birth mom now?" Carrie asked.

Wendy looked down at her notes for a moment and sighed. "We don't know. She was evicted from her apartment, and I was able to find one police report where she was arrested for soliciting. She could be in rehab, or on the streets, or dead for all we know."

Jonathan leaned forward with his arms on the table. "What about Abigail and Logan?"

"They were placed in a foster home—the same one they're in right now, which is a bit of a miracle. Let's see … Logan was hospitalized for four days at first until his infections cleared up and he was healthy enough to go home. At this point he's too young for us to know if there's any permanent damage from the prenatal exposure, or any impact from the poor nutrition during the first few weeks of his life. He's small for his age, but did take his first steps last week," she said with a smile.

Carrie felt her heart drop. *We missed his first steps!*

"He's a bit behind on his milestones, but he is reaching them. As far as the cocaine exposure, there is a risk of hearing loss and learning disabilities. The hearing loss you should begin testing for when he's four, unless you see reason to start earlier. Learning disabilities tend to show up around third grade. The foster parents say that he loves all animals, and is generally a happy child but is easily frightened by loud noises or sudden movement. He frequently gets colds.

"Oh, I should mention that I've met Abigail and Logan personally on two occasions now, for two hours each time. Their guardianship order came through a month ago, but it took time for them to be assigned an adoption worker and then for me to visit them and prepare their file. I also met with the grandparents—they're the ones who gave me the information on birth mom. We had looked into a family placement for the children, but the family is quite closed off to that."

"In some ways Abigail is quite the little lady. She's very protective of her brother—very much like a mother to him. From what I observed, she communicates effectively and has good gross motor skills, but her fine motor skills are quite delayed and she's excellent at avoiding any task she doesn't want to do. She also has moments where she melts down. Picture a two-year-old tantrum in a five-year-old body. I witnessed one the last time I was there and she absolutely wears herself out and then crashes afterward. It was interesting to note that when she crashed, she took herself into a corner and fell asleep, rather than seeking the comfort of her foster mom."

"Is she in therapy at all?" Carrie asked.

"Unfortunately not. The foster parents are wonderful, but they live out of town and the mom doesn't like to drive. Abigail would absolutely benefit from some play therapy, as well as occupational therapy before she starts kindergarten—maybe even after. But none of those are appropriate until she's had some time to bond with her new family. I expect she will offer quite the challenges, at least in the first few months of placement. However, she is very good at communicating and I think this will help immensely. Trust me, this one will let you know what she's thinking!

"Now it's your turn to talk!" Wendy said smiling. "What do you think? How do you feel? What else do you need to know?"

Carrie and Jonathan looked at each other and she gave him a slight nod. "Well," he said, "it's a lot to take in. We were warned about this when we talked to a friend of ours who's a social worker. The thing where you kind of experience a part of everything the kids have already been through and it's heartbreaking and overwhelming. I just

… I'm stuck with a picture in my mind of a little girl sitting in a grungy apartment hallway trying to comfort her baby brother…"

Carrie put her hand on Jonathan's leg and he took it and gripped it tightly. That was exactly what she was thinking about, plus imagining what it must have been like in that apartment, especially for Abigail. Surrounded by adults getting high and passing out. She must've been terrified. Or, maybe that was her normal, which was almost worse to think about.

"What about the foster parents? Don't they want to adopt them?"

"No. When they first took in Abigail and Logan they thought it would be for a few weeks—that's often the time it takes for birth parents to sober up and clean up their place. And the foster dad has been diagnosed with Parkinson's, so this will be their last placement. They care for the children, but they're tired. And with Logan starting to walk there will be a lot more activity coming up."

"So" Jonathan said hesitatingly, "is there any chance you have some pictures of them?"

"Oh, yes! I took these last week and got them printed. Here." She passed over a handful of pictures.

The first one was a close up of the two siblings. Each had big brown eyes, olive skin, and thin, straight hair. Logan was beaming for the camera, his top four teeth visible. Abigail was looking straight at the camera too, but her expression was serious. They slowly looked through the pictures. Logan looking wobbly on two feet, Abigail throwing a stuffie in the air, and one where Abigail was looking at her brother with a big smile on her face.

"Wow," Jonathan said in a breathy voice. "Um, what would be next steps?"

Wendy smiled, "Well, I want you to take at least two days to think about this. Talk with your kids and your family. While these two aren't designated as special needs children, I would think of them as such. They've been though stress and uncertainty with birth mom—

and that's just what we know—they've been apprehended by police, they've been taken from their birth parents and placed with foster parents. That's a lot for any child to deal with. I would recommend being very clear with Matthew and Katie that these two might be very shy at first—even frightened. They're not going to walk into your home and instantly love you all."

"But," she said as she closed the file in front of her, "over time they'll learn to trust you, and then love you. They're children that have had a rough start, but I believe they can have a bright future." She laughed. "OK, I'll get off my soap box now."

Carrie reached over and put her hands over Wendy's. "Thank you for considering us for these kids. It's an honor. We'll do our best to make the right decision for our family." She looked at Jonathan. "Even though I may have to tie Jonathan down when we walk outside so he doesn't float away."

"You two are quite the likeable couple! I can see why Dennis pushed so hard for me to consider you."

They looked at Dennis in surprise. "Hey, she had a big pile of applicants. I just helped her see the right trees in the forest."

For the next two days, every conversation revolved around Abigail and Logan. Carrie tried to warn the kids that any placement like this would have challenges.

"They haven't had the chance to have the same Mommy and Daddy loving them since they were born, like you have," she said while Matthew was setting the table for supper and Katie was sitting at the kitchen island coloring. "And because of that, they might have a really hard time accepting us as family. Or they might accept us and everyone around us as family without any appropriate boundaries."

"What does *that* mean Mommy?"

"Uh, sometimes kids that haven't had a lot of security growing up will try to get love from everyone. Like, they might run up to another mommy at the grocery store and take their hand and start walking out the door with them. It's like they have a really hard time making a deep connection with one person—like a mommy—and at the same time they make a surface connection with everyone."

Matthew paused at the cupboard, "So, like, their brain doesn't know how to bond with a mom the way ours does?"

"Yes, exactly! Now, it's possible that Abigail and Logan aren't like that. But *if* they get placed with us, I want us to be prepared to just accept them wherever they're at. Even if it hurts our feelings. They won't mean to do it, but, like Matthew said, their brain might need time to learn new behaviors."

"Mommy?"

"Yes?"

"Maybe the first time I see them I shouldn't hug them." Katie put down her crayon and put her chin in her hand. She was definitely a hugger.

"You know, I think that's an important thing to keep in mind. We could try to take cues from them. What cues tell you that someone wants a hug?"

"Oh! If they lift up their arms like Alex and Brittany do!"

"Yes," Carrie answered.

"And if they look sad, like Angela did when her Mommy was sick."

"Uh, not so much that one. Believe it or not, some people don't want a hug when they're sad."

"I always want a hug when I'm sad!"

"Other kids may be different than you," Carrie said. She peeked in the oven. The chicken and rice casserole was a perfect golden color and bubbling around the edges. "Supper's ready. Katie, can you go call Daddy from his office?"

Matthew fed Maisy while Katie hollered for her daddy at top volume.

"I hope the kids don't mind noise!" Matthew said.

Once they were seated and eating, they all took turns talking about their day. "I spent a little bit of time today looking at seven passenger vehicles," Jonathan said carefully.

Katie's eyes lit up. "You mean, like a minivan with a button that opens the door? Magnus has one and I looooove it!"

Carrie glared at Jonathan. She had always hated minivans.

He winked at her before answering. "Nope. No minivans for this family. I'm thinking an SUV. And not just if we get the kids. There's no way we can go anywhere with Maisy in either of our cars right now. And when the weather warms up there's lots of places we could take her to play."

"But we don't need three vehicles," Matthew pointed out.

"Noooooo, we don't." He looked at Carrie, but she avoided his gaze and got up to bring the salt and pepper to the table.

"Can I talk about my day now?" Katie asked.

"Sure, after you tell me what color vehicle you think we should get."

"Pink!" she said triumphantly.

"I knew it!" Jonathan said slapping the table. "And *so* not going to happen, darling." Katie's face fell. "Well, maybe we can get a pink sticker to put in the window!"

"Yay!"

Later that night Jonathan brought two glasses of wine up to their loveseat in the bedroom. Carrie took it suspiciously.

"I'm not getting rid of my car. You know that." She had barely survived her old Ford Taurus as a single mom. When she managed to pay back some money she had borrowed from her parents, her dad turned around and used it to upgrade her vehicle to a 2004 Honda Civic. It was more than a reliable car. It was a symbol of her dad's love for her, and how hard they had all worked to get where they were now.

"I know," Jonathan answered, stretching out his legs and sipping his wine.

"It's still a good car," she insisted, feeling compelled to prove her point. "It's been perfectly maintained, it's pretty good on gas. Well, not like it's electric or anything, but still! And the paint job is in great shape. I mean, sure it's small. We wouldn't be able to take Maisy anywhere. But it makes a good car for me to take around town. That's all I need for driving the kids places! Matthew's safe to sit in the front, and Katie can sit in the back between the kids—if they come of course. Hey, we're going to need a car seat for Logan. Abigail can use Katie's old booster seat…" her voice trailed off.

Jonathan didn't say anything. He reached over and held Carrie's free hand while he continued to slowly drink his wine.

She couldn't ignore the facts. A car seat and a booster seat in the back would make it really crowded. Katie would probably even have trouble buckling her seat belt. And the car didn't have side impact bags. It hadn't bothered her until she started dating Jonathan who had big issues about car safety. He had tried a few times to convince Carrie to buy a safer car, but at the time she couldn't afford it.

That was no longer a reason. And she knew why he always suggested she drive his car—it was safer.

"Could we keep it for Matthew to learn on?" she asked in a small voice.

"If you really want to, of course we can."

"But…" she prompted.

"But I was wondering if one of the clients at the women's center you used to volunteer at could use a car. We would only get about a thousand for it max, and we're still a few years away from Matthew driving, but for someone without a car it could change their life."

Carrie turned to face him. "Geez. You know exactly what to say to make me think about changing my mind."

He looked at her earnestly. "I don't want you to feel pushed, though. Yes, I have a lot of good points, and I know what that car means to you."

She took a deep breath. "OK. I can do this. With your help. I'll call Donna, the director at the center tomorrow and see what she thinks."

He lifted up her hand and kissed the back of it. "Letting things from the past go to make room for the future. Isn't that what you tell your clients?"

She rolled her eyes. "Yes. Don't rub it in."

"What kind of car do you want?" He paused. "Too soon?"

She nodded. "Too soon."

CHAPTER 32

"Carrie! How nice to hear from you! How is everything?" Donna asked.

Carrie paused to adjust the phone under her ear while she mixed cookies. "Good! I've passed my provisionals and I'm now a fully licensed counseling psychologist."

"Where are you working?"

The center where Carrie had done part of her practicum had asked her to continue on as a volunteer at the end of her contract, but she had declined. Their paid psychologist, Dr. Bradley, had been extremely difficult to work under, and with his connections to the board there was no chance she'd be offered his job.

"I'm at the clinic one full day a week and I have private clients that I meet online from home three days a week."

"What a great idea! You know, I don't think a week goes by that someone doesn't bring up your name. The girls still ask each other 'how's that working for you' and I've seen those little envelopes with their dreams and goals inside more times than I can count."

Carrie smiled. It had been a tough road to earn the trust of women who saw her as privileged and out-of-touch, but as they got to know her—and she got to know them—they began to not only listen to her, but to try the things she was suggesting.

"We do have one casualty from your time here," Donna went on. Carrie's heart dropped. What had gone wrong? "You'll remember Pamela, our receptionist? Well, she's now back in school full-time to become an electrician, of all things! When she handed in her resignation she said it was all because of you. I'm still looking for the right replacement."

"She did it? Oh wow. That's amazing! We only had one or two conversations about that before I left. Can you even imagine how busy she's going to be as a mature female electrician? I wish I knew someone I could recommend to take her place. If I think of anyone I'll let you know. But there's another reason I called. I have an old, but well-maintained Honda Civic. Our family's growing and it's time to get a bigger car. Do you know anyone at the center we could gift the car to? It's nothing fancy, but it runs well."

"You're expecting? Oh Carrie, how exciting!"

"Expecting, yes, but not in the traditional sense. Jonathan and I have been approved to adopt. We're in the process of possibly adopting two children—a five-year-old girl and her one-year-old brother. Thus the need for a bigger vehicle!"

There was a long pause. "Are you sure about this? Those kids will come with lots of challenges."

Carrie tried to remain calm. "Well, they haven't had all the privileges my older kids have had, but we're ready to give them the best possible chance. What do you think about the car?"

"Oh, that's easy. You remember Char?"

"Of course! When I finished my practicum she was about to enroll in an early childhood education program." Carrie also remembered that Char had been difficult to connect with for quite a while, but had slowly come around, even to the point of introducing Carrie to her boyfriend. Carrie had worked with both of them and encouraged the boyfriend to take an anger management course, which he had.

"Well, she's quite the success story. She won't graduate until June, but one of the preschools she did a practicum in has already offered her a job for the fall when one of their full time teachers retires."

"Wow, that's fantastic! She must be so excited!"

"Well she hasn't accepted yet, because she doesn't have a way of getting there for nine in the morning. It's in the suburbs and the bus system leaves a lot to be desired. For her practicum they allowed her to start at ten, but that won't do in the fall."

"And she has her license?"

"She does. For a while she was borrowing her boyfriend's car, but it broke down about a month ago. But I have to say, nothing has deterred her from pushing towards that goal of being a preschool teacher."

"That's settled then. Is there a regular time that she's at the center? I can bring the car to her then and have Jonathan come to give me a ride home after."

"Yes, the girls all meet on Wednesday evenings now."

"Dr. Bradley does an evening session?" Carrie couldn't picture the grumpy psychologist ever working a full day, let alone an evening.

"No!" Donna chuckled. "He didn't get a brain transplant. The girls do this on their own. A few of them bought that book *Take Control of Your Life* and they work through it together every week."

Carrie stopped mixing and went and sat down at the island. Leaving the center had been a difficult decision because she didn't want to leave all the women there in the lurch. To know they were doing so well, and taking action on their own, was the best news she could have imagined.

"Oh Donna. You don't even know how happy that makes me. Wow. OK, so what would be the best way to do this? Should I maybe come at the end of the session? I don't want to interrupt what they're doing."

"Yes, that's a good idea. Security locks up at nine, so if you're there at 8:30 when they're wrapping up you'll have a chance to see the others and then talk to Char. She's always the last one to leave."

"Great! I'll be there at 8:30 tomorrow night!"

"This is a really good thing you're doing Carrie, thank you!"

Carrie ended the call and went to start putting cookies in the oven. Then it hit her. She was getting rid of her car. Tomorrow. She ran downstairs to where Jonathan was working. He turned around with a big smile.

"Couldn't stand to be away from me a second longer?"

"No. Yes. Maybe. Um, we're giving the car to Char at the center. Tomorrow night."

He leaned back in his chair. "What? That's amazing! I shouldn't be surprised, but dang! You moved fast!"

"Is that OK? Can we make it with just your car until we get another vehicle? After I hung up I realized I shouldn't have been so hasty. Maybe move it to next week?"

"Nope. This is good. I have an idea of which vehicle I want. Can we go now and look at it? I can finish up work later tonight."

"I already promised Kara I could watch Magnus today after school. And Matthew's got LGBT club so he can't babysit. We could bring the kids with us I guess. Wait. Weren't you going to trade in your car? That still leaves us with only one vehicle."

He smacked his head. "Right. Forgot about that. Still, we do need to get a bigger vehicle ASAP. I say we do this today and manage with one vehicle."

"I guess I'm baking cookies to go then. Do you need to make an appointment at the dealer?"

"Yeah, I'll do that right now and then take Maisy for her walk so we can go straight from school."

"Alright. Holler up if that's a go so I can leave a message for Katie and Magnus to meet us in the pick-up lane."

CHAPTER 33

"I feel like I need to just sit here for a moment and try to stop my head from spinning," Carrie admitted. They had arrived early at the center in their separate vehicles, and then Jonathan had come to sit with her in the Civic until it was time to go in.

"It's weird how things happen," he admitted. "It's like going to buy the new vehicle yesterday broke through some sort of barrier."

On their way home from the dealer in their new-to-them, seven-seater SUV with all the bells, whistles, and safety features, Dennis had called. Everything was ready for them to meet Abigail and Logan as the first step in the adoption. The meeting was set for Thursday at four at Wendy's office.

Matthew had come home from club to find a new vehicle and a date to meet his new brother and sister. It was a lot to process.

Then today, while Carrie worked a full day at the clinic, Jonathan had scrambled to get the bill of sale ready for Char, and pay for a year's insurance so she wouldn't be suddenly saddled with more expenses than she could handle.

Now they were about to give a car away and then go home to count the minutes until they all met Abigail and Logan for the first time.

"Yeah. It all feels a bit unreal at this point." Jonathan reached up and affectionately ran his hand across the dash. "Have you said your goodbyes to this old friend?"

"Yep. I spent the ride over thanking this car for its service and promising that the new owner would be very good to it. I hope I didn't oversell things!" she joked. "OK, looks like it's time to go in. Are you sure you don't want to come?"

He nodded. "These are your people. Go enjoy some time with them. I'll wait here for when you bring Char out to see her car."

"Okey dokey." She patted the steering wheel and then got out. Maybe she would've felt more emotional about the whole thing under different circumstances. But with the meeting with Abigail and Logan coming tomorrow, everything else —including sentimental attachments to old cars—seemed a lot less important than a few days ago.

She pressed the buzzer at the side door and waited to be let in. Security was important in this neighborhood, and for some of the clients who used the center. Carrie knew someone would check carefully before opening the door. She just hoped it was someone who would recognize her.

The door swung open and Char was standing there beaming. "Carrie!" she shouted, throwing her arms around her. "Oh my gosh! Come in! Everyone's gonna flip!" She closed the door and waited for it to click and then grabbed Carrie's hand.

Laughing Carrie allowed herself to be dragged into the room where she had spent so many group sessions. About half the faces looked familiar and they all jumped up to hug her. It was a far cry from her first session where no one even acknowledged her presence for the first five minutes!

"We were just finishing up," Char said. "We do this thing every week where we each say one new thing we learned during the session. Are you OK if we still do that?"

"Yes, of course!"

By the end Carrie was wiping tears from her eyes. She shouldn't be surprised. The program they were using was one of the best for inspiring real lasting change. But to hear how everyone was taking responsibility for their behavior, their circumstances, and their future was overwhelming.

At 8:45, everyone quickly started gathering their bags and jackets. "Our buses come between 8:50 and nine," Char explained, "so we all go out together to wait at the stop. You know, safety in numbers and all that. Security's probably waiting outside to lock up."

"Oh, well, can I drive you home tonight? I'd love to chat for a few more minutes."

"Yeah, sure." Char made sure everyone was together before following them outside with Carrie. Sure enough, a man in a yellow jacket with 'ALL-SIDE SECURITY' in black letters on the back was waiting for them.

"Chester, I'm going home with Carrie here, she's parked out back."

He locked the doors and double checked them. "No problem Char. I'll walk you both back. There's a guy sitting in a car back there. He said he was waiting for one of you."

"Oh, that's my husband Jonathan," Carrie explained. But Chester still walked back and watched them until Jonathan waved to him from the SUV.

"Here, pop in the driver's seat of my car," Carrie insisted. Char gave her a confused look, but complied. Carrie got in on the passenger side and shut the door.

"So, I called Donna the other day, and she said you've already been offered a job as a preschool teacher!"

"Yeah, it's pretty cool. It's in this super fancy neighborhood but I love it! I'm probably going to have to turn it down, though. With all the transfers to take the bus there I can't make it by the time the school opens."

"Do you have your license?"

"Actually I do. One thing my dad did for me, I guess. Just no car."

Carrie took the car keys and held them out. "Here you go. This is your car now. It's not fancy but it will get you from A to B. The tank is full, it's recently had an oil change and a tune up from my dad who's a retired mechanic, and the insurance is paid for a year."

"Holy fu… sh… I mean… Whoa. Are you for real?" She reached for the keys with a shaking hand and then pulled back her hand and tucked it under her leg.

"Yes. Jonathan," Carrie pointed to him waiting in the car and he gave a little wave, "and I are doing really good right now. In fact, we're hoping to adopt two little kids, and this car is way too small for us. I'm ridiculously sentimental about it because my Dad gave it to me when I was really struggling, and I didn't want it to go to just anyone. I asked Donna who could use it, and when she suggested you, I knew it was the right thing. I got help when I needed it, and now I get to pass that on."

"No way," Char breathed, and this time she held her hand out and accepted the keys from Carrie. "Seriously, today was the worst. Just before we had our meeting my mom called. I know better than to answer, but I just had a brain lapse for a second. She was drunk. As usual. And she was just like, 'you might actually graduate but you'll be out on the streets whoring yourself in no time'."

"That's horrible!"

"She always has this way of tearing me down before I get the chance to stand on my feet, you know? But now … oh my God Carrie. Now I can accept that job! And they said I might even be able to work at the daycare center next door in the summer until preschool starts!"

She reached across and gave Carrie an enthusiastic hug. "This is the BEST!"

"I'm so happy for you. You've worked really hard to get here, and now just think of all the little lives you're going to make better in your job! OK, so we've already done all the transfer papers. I hope it's OK that Donna gave me some of your info so I could fill it out."

"Yeah, totally!"

"Here you go then. Keep this in the glove box. It's your proof of insurance. And about a month before it expires you'll want to start shopping around for the best rates for next year. Also, there's a folder in the backseat with the entire repair history since I got it—you can thank my dad for that part."

"This is crazy! I have a car! You just freakin' gave me a freakin' car!"

Carrie grinned. "Yep. Are you OK to drive home?"

"Oh yeah. Man, Damien is going to FLIP OUT when he finds out!"

"Well, I'll let you head home so he can start flipping! And remember Char, you're doing an amazing job at creating your own future *and* it's going to be a good future! Not to mention all the good you're doing with everyone you meet with here. Your mom doesn't see the real you right now, but I'm so, so, SO proud of you!" She reached over to hug Char again, then said goodbye and got into Jonathan's car.

The last thing they saw was Char fist pumping the air as she drove away.

"Do you think she's happy?" Jonathan joked.

"Maybe just a teeny, tiny, massive amount. And that was the most fun I've had in a while!"

CHAPTER 34

"OK, nice big slow breaths everyone," Carrie said as they pulled into a parking spot. It was like going to the hospital to have a baby—except it wouldn't be the most physically painful experience of her life, and she already know the gender, the names, and what these children looked like.

She turned around to look at Matthew and Katie. Matthew had his eyes closed and was breathing in and out slowly. Katie was bouncing up and down in her seat with her arms wrapped tightly around herself.

"Whatcha' doing Katie-girl?"

"I'm getting all my hugs in now so I don't give any away if nobody wants them!"

"Oh, good idea. Well, let's go see Abigail and Logan!"

She exchanged nervous smiles with Jonathan as they got out of their SUV. Together they made their way through the lobby and into the elevator. Another man followed them in and smiled.

"I'm going to see my maybe new sister and brother!" Katie announced to him.

"Well, that must be exciting," he said, still smiling. "Congratulations!"

They got off on the fourth floor and Katie say 'bye' and waved to the man as they walked to the reception desk.

"Hi, we're here to meet with Wendy," Jonathan said.

"And Logan and Abigail!" Katie added.

Seconds later Wendy was walking down the hall towards them. "Hello everyone!" She reached out her hand to Matthew. "I'm Wendy."

He shook her hand firmly. "Hi, I'm Matthew."

Then she crouched down to Katie's level. "Hello, I'm Wendy."

"Are you showing us Abigail and Logan?"

"Yes. What do you think about that?"

"I think I want to see them now and not talk about it anymore." Katie nodded her head. "We've talked about it *a lot*."

Wendy laughed. "Well, I have a few things to talk about first, but I'll keep it short. Let's have a seat here in the lobby."

Katie wedged herself between Carrie and Jonathan when they sat down.

"First of all, Dennis had planned to be here but an emergency came up and he can't make it. He does apologize, but these things happen often in our world. So, Abigail and Logan and their foster parents are here in one of our family rooms. They brought some toys along that they enjoy playing with, and they know that they're going to meet some special people soon. They don't know any more than that."

She paused to look at each of them. "Please don't make any statements about being their new family or anything like that. Let's just give them some unpressured time to get used to being around you, OK?"

They all nodded.

"And please keep your phones and cameras put away. These children are wards of the court, and we need to protect their privacy until they are legally adopted. That means continuing to not mention their names on any social media sites and not sharing any images of them. That's it! Let's go say hello."

The walk down the hallway felt like a mile to Carrie. She could hear the sounds of a little girl chattering, and it felt surreal to wonder if that was her daughter's voice. A baby babble answered and she knew it must be Abigail and Logan.

Wendy opened the door slowly and walked in. "Hello again. I'd like you to meet my friends." She turned sideways as Carrie, Jonathan, Katie, and Matthew walked in.

"This is Carrie the mom, and this is Jonathan the dad, and this is Katie and Matthew!" She walked over and crouched beside Abigail who had stopped mid-sentence when they walked in and was now staring at them. "This is Abigail, and Logan"—Wendy stood up and put a hand on the shoulders of an older couple sitting on chairs facing the play area—"and Henry and Sandra."

They all said hi to the kids, and Jonathan and Carrie reached out and shook Henry and Sandra's hands. Carrie was briefly aware of Henry's left hand shaking in his lap before she turned to the kids.

Abigail didn't say anything, but she moved closer to Logan. He was standing in front of a low table, hanging on to the edge with one hand and wobbling a little. He gave them a big smile and then turned back to a colorful plastic dog in his hand that made noises whenever he touched its back. His wispy brown hair fell to the side in the front, just missing his bright brown eyes. He was wearing a grey t-shirt and blue jogging pants with little Velcro sneakers.

Katie slowly came over and kneeled beside him. He held out the toy to her. She touched its back and Logan giggled when it made a barking noise.

"That's my brudder," Abigail said. Her hair hung down to her shoulders and she brushed it back with the palm of her hand when she leaned forward. She was wearing a pink dress that looked a little small, pink leggings, and sneakers similar to her brother's.

Katie pointed up at Matthew who was still standing by the door. "That's *my* brother."

"Oh."

Carrie, Jonathan, and Matthew carefully sat down on the couch behind the children and Abigail turned, as if to avoid having them behind her.

"I'm five," she said to Matthew.

"I'm twelve," he answered. "But I'll be thirteen soon. When's your birthday?"

Abigail squeezed her eyes together for a moment, before turning to the adults at the table. "Sandra, what's my birfday?"

"It's June 25th dear. You'll be six years old!"

She turned back to Matthew, "I be six!"

"Wow. That's pretty old. What do you want for your birthday?"

"New brudder. Logan's little."

Jonathan coughed to hide his laugh. The sound got Logan's attention and he reached over to Jonathan's knee before shuffle-walking the foot to him. He kept his hand on Jonathan's knee and looked at him intensely. Jonathan pretended to cough again and Logan copied him.

"So, Jonathan. What do you do?" Henry asked.

Jonathan reluctantly pulled his attention away from Logan. "I have a private internet security firm. And Carrie's a psychologist. How 'bout you?"

"Well, I used to be a police officer." He held up his shaking hand. "Retired. Parkinson's."

"Ah, that's a rough diagnosis."

"You got that right."

"Do you work full-time then?" Sandra asked looking at Carrie.

"Yes and no. I have online clients that I see from my home office a few days a week and I work at a clinic one day a week." She put her hand on Jonathan's free knee. "Jonathan works from home most of the time so there's always one of us there." She wanted to ask Sandra questions about the kids, but wasn't sure what would be appropriate.

"Sandra," Wendy spoke up, "why don't you share with us what a typical day is with the kids."

"Oh, of course! Well, they both wake up early—sometimes even seven o'clock! But they stay in their beds and play until eight. Abigail is very good at getting Logan up and dressed. They share a room. For breakfast they do like their sweet cereals. Lucky Charms is the favorite right now."

"You get Lucky Charms?" Katie asked Abigail.

"Uh huh." Abigail nodded.

"Lucky. Daddy used to give us Lucky Charms when Mommy went away, but now we have to have healthy breakfasts." She made a face and Abigail giggled. "Wanna do that puzzle?" she asked, pointing to a puzzle sticking out of a bag.

"No. I no like puzzles. They's Wendy's."

"You can do it if you like, Katie." Wendy offered. Katie went and got out the puzzle and set it on the low table.

"Logan bites puzzles," Abigail warned.

"Oh," Katie's face fell and she went and put the puzzle back. "Well is there something we can play that Logan won't bite?"

"I read you a book and not let Logan bite it!" Abigail pulled out a board book from a different bag and set it on the table out of Logan's reach. She opened to the first page and started to 'read' but it was immediately obvious she was making up a story.

"Hey," Katie started, and Carrie quickly held up a warning hand and shook her head 'no'.

"Anyways," Sandra went on, "They like to watch TV in the mornings. Then after lunch they both go down for a nap. It usually ends up being play time, but they know to stay in their room until two. I have a digital clock in there and Abigail can tell time. If the weather's nice we might go for a walk. It's getting a bit harder because Logan wants to try walking instead of staying in his stroller. We like to sit on a bench at the pond and watch the ducks. After supper they watch videos. We're still a VHS family and we've got lots of kids' shows. And then bedtime at seven."

"Oh." Carrie was at a loss for what to say. "Abigail, would you read your story again to me?"

"OK!" She grabbed her book and climbed onto the couch beside Carrie and opened the book. "That's a bad girl. She not good. She not help. Mommy say, 'go away'! The little girl goed to the forest. She finded a big bear. She said, 'be my friend'! Bear said, 'OK but you have to sleep in my cave'. The girl said, 'I like caves' and they be friends!"

"Hey, I really like the ending to the book!" Carrie felt her breath catch as Abigail leaned against her just a little bit. "What's your favorite color?"

"Pink!"

"Me too!" Katie said with a big smile. "We're like sisters!" Then her face fell and she bit her lip and looked at Wendy. "Sorry."

"It's OK, Katie. I think it's so fun that you both like pink! What else do you like?"

"I like school, and gymnastics, and swimming, and Maisy, and Angela, and baby Brielle, and baby Alex!"

"Wow! You must be very busy!"

"Yep. Oh, and musical theater because my Daddy says I'm very traumatic."

"Dramatic, Katie. Dramatic." Jonathan said.

Katie giggled. "What do *you* like Abigail?"

"I like ice cweam. I eat ice cweam ever day!"

"Abigail," Sandra said in a firm voice. "You can't make things up."

Abigail's mouth turned down.

Henry leaned over and said something to Sandra.

"I think we need to get going," Sandra said. "This isn't a good time for Henry because his meds are wearing off."

"Oh, I'm so sorry," Carrie said. "Please, next time you choose what's best for you. We have a flexible schedule."

"Thank you. Abigail, put the things back in the bag." She stood up and looked at Wendy. "Could you bring in the stroller and our jackets?"

"Oh, yes, of course." A few seconds later she was back with a stroller.

Abigail picked up a little blue jacket and put it on Logan without zipping it up. Then she put on her own jacket. Sandra picked up Logan and wrestled him into the stroller as he squirmed and protested. Once he was buckled, she helped Henry up, put his coat on, and zipped it up. Then she got her own coat on. "It was very nice to meet you all. I hope things work out quickly. I need to focus on Henry's care."

Henry raised his good hand in a good-bye and then they were out the door.

"I'll be right back," Wendy said, following them out.

It was almost ten minutes later when she returned. "So sorry to keep you waiting. I wanted to make sure they got loaded into the car OK. By the time we were on the main floor Henry was having difficulty lifting up his feet and Sandra needed to almost pull him along." She paused and took a deep breath. "I'm shocked at how much he's deteriorated."

"Could it maybe just be the time of day? Like Sandra said?" Carrie asked.

"Maybe." She sat down in the chair Sandra had been sitting in. "So, tell me how you think that went."

"I like them! They should come live with us soon so they can play and go to school and have fun. They spend toooooo much time watching TV!" Katie said adamantly.

"You may have a point, Katie. What about the rest of you?"

"It was pretty hard not to pick up Logan," Jonathan admitted. "Especially when he was looking up at me with those big eyes! But other than that I think it went really well for the short time we saw them. I mean, at least we didn't scare them or anything!"

"It would be interesting to see how Logan responds to being picked up. I don't think Sandra and Henry pick him up much!" Wendy mused.

"I thought it went good," Matthew said slowly. "But isn't it going to be super scary for them to be in a new home with new people and new rules?"

"Yes. It might be. Or it might be a welcome change for them. They certainly look to Sandra to provide for their needs, but ..." Wendy's voice trailed off.

Carrie gently touched the spot where Abigail had been sitting. "Well, I can say that I've fallen completely in love with them, but there are going to be some big challenges. Even just how busy our days are compared to what they're used to. Plus, like Katie said, we sure don't watch that much TV! And I really want to give Abigail a chance to just be a little girl, but I can't see her relinquishing her mothering of Logan. She doesn't really change his diapers, does she?"

"I'm afraid so. I know it seems shocking, but learning responsibility and independence is key to surviving the foster system. So is taking care of others."

"Well, that's not how we do things," Jonathan said. "Sure, the kids have responsibilities but we draw the line at parenting each other!"

"And that's something you can work toward," Wendy promised. "Well, I think we've given you even more things to talk about." She looked at Katie. "Sorry about that."

"It's OK," Katie answered. "I like talking, I just don't like listening to everyone else talking!"

"A girl after my own heart!" Wendy said with a smile. "I'll be in touch with you in the next day or so and we'll go from there." She stood up. "Do you need me to walk you out?"

They all stood up. "We can make our own way out. Thank you for setting this up Wendy." Carrie said. "They really are very special children."

CHAPTER 35

As Carrie went to sleep that night her mind was filled with thoughts of Abigail and Logan. They had agreed that the kids should continue to share a room—if they were actually placed with them. Matthew would move to the guest room and let them have his room. When guests came he could sleep in the living room or basement.

They had gone out for supper after the meeting, and she was keenly aware that they might not have very many more dinners out as just the four of them. She wondered if the other kids had even gone out to a restaurant. Sandra and Henry didn't exactly seem like the type to plan outings of any type. Did they know about McDonald's? Had they ever been swimming? Or to the beach?

The next morning she woke up instantly when the alarm went off, her thoughts running to all the things they should be doing to get ready. Again, *if* they were placed with them. She needed to find out what kind of bed each of them slept on. They needed bedding, clothes, a car seat for Logan, maybe a wagon instead of a stroller? He obviously wanted to be out and about, not buckled in a stroller!

What about stimulating toys? And should she look into preschools for Abigail? What about a Baby and Me class for Logan? Jaz took Alex to a bunch of activities like that. She'd need to text Jaz once they knew for sure the kids were coming. Right. *If* they were coming.

After her coffee was ready, she sat down at the table facing the big sliding door out to the backyard. Jonathan had put up a play structure for the kids before they got married. That would get a lot of use in the spring…

She gave her head a shake. It was a lot to take in. She needed to center herself and calm down. With such young kids the transition could take months. Closing her eyes, she focused on slowing her breathing and saying, 'I love myself'. When she felt centered, she focused on thinking about how much she loved her family and her friends.

"Mommy? Are you editing?" A tiny voice asked.

Carrie opened her eyes. "You mean meditating? Yes, I was. Come here." Katie climbed into her lap. "I was meditating on how much I love you and all my family and friends."

Katie wrapped her arms around Carrie. "I love you too Mommy."

They sat like that for a few more minutes until they heard Jonathan's voice as he walked down the stairs. "No problem. Yes, we're both up … Oh. Wow. Uh …" he rubbed his hand across his forehead and then through his hair. "Um. OK. We'll talk about it and call you back … Yes, I understand. Thank you. Bye."

He walked into the kitchen and held up Carrie's phone. "You left this on your night table and it was ringing. Uh, that was Wendy. It involves all of us so I'm going to go wake up Matthew."

Carrie's heart sank. "I'll make you a coffee."

Jonathan turned to give her a grateful look before jogging up the stairs. Soon, they were all sitting at the table.

"So, Wendy called this morning. Did you kids notice that Henry's hand was shaking during our visit yesterday?"

"Yeah! He was really nervous!"

Jonathan reached over and ruffled Katie's hair. "Actually, he wasn't nervous. Henry has something called Parkinson's Disease. It can make the body shake like that."

"But Daddy! You shook his hand! Now you'll get it."

"No Katie. It's not contagious. You can't get it from someone else. But it does make it really hard for the person who has it to move around. Wendy was very concerned about him, and she went to visit them at their house last night after the kids were in bed. They admitted that it's too much for them to have the kids. So, either they go to another foster home until the adoption placement is complete, or they get placed with us. On Monday."

There was a minute of stunned silence before Katie jumped up. "YAY!!! My sister AND my brother are coming on Monday!!!!! Woooohoooo!!!" She ran around the table twice before Jonathan caught her and placed her in his lap.

"Hang on Katie-girl. Let's talk this through. Wendy said that even if they go to another foster family, they will still get placed with us eventually if we want them. And we agreed at supper last night that we absolutely want them."

"But," Matthew said with a worried look, "then they'd be in a new home with new rules and new people only to be moved again. That's not good for them.

Carrie put her arm around his hunched shoulders. "What do you think we should do?"

"I think we should have them come straight here. Even if it's hard for a bit, it's better than them getting thrown around to different homes. And, well maybe I shouldn't say this. But I don't think a foster family will *love* them like a forever family will."

Carrie looked at Jonathan.

"I say Monday too. It would kill me to think they're out there some-where with strangers."

"Then I'll call Wendy back and tell her to bring them on Monday." She picked up the phone to dial, but needed to take a minute before her hands stopped shaking enough to press Wendy's number. "I'm shaking from excitement, just so you all know."

"Hi, Wendy? It's Carrie here. We've talked it over as a family, and we'd love to have Abigail and Logan join our family on Monday." She smiled. "Thank you. It's very exciting for us, too! ... I do have a few questions. Um, I'll probably call you a few times today." She mimed writing and Matthew jumped up and brought her the notepad they used to write groceries on.

"What kind of beds are they sleeping on? ... OK ... And what size diapers does Logan use?... They will? That's great! The only other thing I can think of right now is do you know how old his car seat is?... Ok. Sure. So we'll need to know his weight so we can get a car seat for him. Right. OK. Oh! What size clothes do they wear? ... Sure. Well, I'm sure we'll talk again soon! Bye."

"What did she say Mommy? What did she say?"

"Let's see. Abigail sleeps on a mattress on the floor, and Logan's still in a crib. Um, my goodness my writing's hard to read! Oh, right. Henry and Sandra aren't giving away their car seat for Logan since they bought it themselves, so Wendy will use a loaner from the office to bring him here—we'll need one pretty quick then." She squinted at her notes. "Logan is only 17 pounds. He wears 9-12 month clothes and Abigail wears size 4T or 5T."

Carrie looked up. "Katie, I think the clothes you've outgrown will be perfect for Abigail. We'll look through them and bring up everything that might fit."

Jonathan finished his coffee and got up to make another one. "You want one Carrie?"

"No, I'm buzzed enough as it is!"

"Well, I have to say I'm not OK with any child sleeping on the floor, even if it's what she's used to. Can we find her a cute bed that's low to the floor or something?"

"Her favorite color is pink, Daddy! We should get Abigail a pink bed."

Jonathan snapped his fingers, "That's it! A pink big girl bed for Abigail."

"I think we should stick to a crib for Logan though. At least for now. Hey! I wonder if Jaz still has Alex's? Maybe we could borrow it for a few months. I'm sure that's all he'll need. You know what guys? This is a pretty big deal in a really short amount of time. We've got to move Matthew to the guest room, set up that room for Abigail and Logan, child proof the whole house. I suggest we call all our friends and get reinforcements."

Jonathan sat down with a fresh cup of coffee. "Is it too early to call your parents and Tom and Martha? As grandparents, they should hear first."

"Wow. I can't believe I forgot that. Yes, thank you." She looked at the time on her phone. "Dad and Mom are probably awake but still in bed. Let's try to FaceTime Tom and Martha first. It's two hours later there. Then we can get Dad and Mom."

Both sets of parents were suitably shocked at the speed things were moving, and sad they couldn't be there to help get things ready.

"Care Bear," Carrie's mom said, "I'd just be in the way right now. But maybe in a couple of weeks when the kids have settled in a little we can come down for a visit. Your dad and I need to start looking at houses anyways, so we can get in some regular visits and let the kids get used to us."

"That sounds perfect Mom, thank you."

"Well, I'd love to hear about everything, but I think you need to get off the phone and start getting ready for my new grandchildren!"

"Bye Grandma!" Katie and Matthew both called out while Carrie and Jonathan waved until the screen went dark.

"Now," Carrie said. "How do we tell everyone at once?"

"Divide and conquer! You take half the list and I take half the list and we start calling. You'd better start with your sister, though, and I'll start with Max."

All of their friends who were local agreed they needed to meet in person to make a game plan. An hour later their house was swarming with people and kids, even though it was just past nine on a Saturday. Even Ken had assigned his assistant coach to the rugby practice and dropped of the older boys so he could be part of the preparations.

Somehow Maria managed to buy enough pastries from the bakery for everyone to have breakfast, and Jonathan was making rapid-fire coffees to order. When they were all crammed into the living room eating and drinking, Kara spoke up.

"Alright everyone. What we have here is a bona fide opportunity to cram nine months of pregnancy times two into less than 48 hours! We each need to focus on what we're good at so this can come together in the shortest amount of time. So Jonathan and Carrie, what's most important for you?"

"Carrie, you've got this," Jonathan said, gesturing to her with his mug.

"OK. I think it's getting Matthew's stuff moved to the guest room and getting the kids' room set up."

"Great. Everyone have their phones out taking notes? Excellent. Well, Max and Jenny have moved your stuff for you once already so they have the most experience. Can I make you guys in charge of getting Matthew set up?"

They nodded.

"And Matthew, this is your stuff, so you're the boss of Uncle Max and Aunty Jenny. Keep them in line."

"Cool!" he answered with a huge smile.

"OK. Next is setting up the kids' room. Jonathan and Carrie, I think you should go out on a little shopping date to choose Abigail's bed and bedding. You *are* the expectant couple now!"

Katie pouted. "I wanted to pick Abigail's bed!"

"I have a different job for you Katie. It's really important."

"OK!"

Kara took a drink of her coffee. "What's next?"

"Well, we need a crib for Logan. Jaz, do you still have Alex's old crib?" Carrie asked.

"Wow, good timing! My parents were just talking about donating it because they don't want it in their garage anymore. I'll get Dad to bring it over, but you'll need bedding because I'm still using Alex's on his toddler bed. And I've got all of his old clothes. What size is Logan?"

Jonathan gave Carrie a thumbs up. "Sweet! Our boy's gonna be stylin'! He's 9-12 months. Whatever that means."

They all laughed and he shrugged. "First baby! What do I know?"

"Let's keep focused here people," Kara joked. "Now, Ken and I want to take Matthew and Katie out shopping for some fun things for the kids' room and maybe some new toys too. Does that sound like a job you can handle Katie?"

"YES!" she shouted, and Alex screamed in response. Jaz quickly quieted him. "Sorry guys. I can't seem to find his volume control anymore."

Lisa laughed, "That boy has never had a volume control. He's just figured out how to be even louder. I love it! Hey Kara, what's my job?"

"Well, since you have the most recent experience child proofing, I wondered if you and your mom could do that here?"

"On it! I have tons of extra supplies from when Alex lived with us. We should be able to do the whole house without going to the store!"

"And I'll take care of ordering in supper for your family for today and tomorrow," Maria added. "You don't need to be worrying about meals when you're about to deliver two children!"

"You're the best!" Jonathan said.

"And I've already got mine and Dustin's job set." Lauren said. "We're taking all your inventory, Carrie, and I'll handle the sales and shipping for the next few weeks. You'll probably be all baby brain anyways and ship the Seattle order to Africa or something."

"Seriously? But you hate all that stuff!"

"And that's how much I love ya babe. I've still got my notes from when you taught me everything so I'll only bug you if I really screw up."

Kara typed some notes into her phone. "I think that's it for the most immediate things. Anything we missed?"

Carrie and Jonathan looked at each other and shook their heads. "Guys, I can't even tell you how much this means to us." Carrie said, trying not to get choked up. "I mean, there's even a possibility we'll get some sleep before Monday now! But more than that, to have you all here, excited about this next chapter in our lives, makes me feel so blessed."

"And if you ever feel overwhelmed, you make sure to ask for help," Jaz said. "Between all of us there will always be someone who can come over right away. And if you need help driving Matthew and

Katie around, or getting groceries, or anything you have to *promise* you'll call."

Carrie put her hand over her heart. "I promise."

Kara looked at her watch. "Alright. I'm giving you all fifteen minutes to chat and then it's time to get to work folks!"

CHAPTER 36

Carrie was up even earlier than usual on Monday morning. She went downstairs to make a cup of coffee and found she couldn't sit still to drink it. So she transferred her coffee to a travel mug. Standing at the sliding door looking out onto the dark yard she tried to imagine it with all the kids out there, playing. Maisy padded over to her and she reached down and pet her. "Not long girl, and you'll have more kids to play with." Maisy wagged her tail.

Carrie walked past the table where a highchair and booster seat had been added, and tried unsuccessfully to remember who had brought them. Walking into the living room she turned on the lights over the TV and fireplace.

In the warm glow she could see their coffee table, which now had colorful children's books on it and rubber edges on all the corners. There was a childproof fence around the fireplace and all the breakables and books on the lower shelves on either side of the fireplace were now set up nicely on higher shelves.

A childproof handle was on the door to the basement, and another fence had been put around the bottom of the stairs leading up to the bedrooms. The wheelchair lift had added a bit of a challenge since they couldn't put a gate across the stair opening. Jenny found a solution online that allowed them to put a fence around the entire set-up with a gate that even Abigail could easily open and had ordered it with rush shipping. Jonathan and Max installed it last night.

Unfortunately, the fence also prevented wheelchair access to the stairs. They'd need a better solution before Carrie's mom could spend the night. But at least the main floor bathroom was wheelchair accessible, so she or Maria could still be comfortable when they were visiting.

Carrie walked through the open gate and up the stairs with Maisy following her. While she couldn't see them in the dark, she knew that every outlet was covered with a safety plug now. All of the kitchen cupboards were safety-latched except for the pots and the plastics, and the bathroom doors all had childproof handles. Katie had practiced mastering them all weekend.

After standing outside Matthew and Katie's bedroom doors and listening to their deep breathing, Carrie turned on the light in the new kids' room. She walked in and sat on Abigail's new bed.

Kara had been right. Shopping for Abigail's bed was a special time for her and Jonathan in the midst of all the busy running around. They had gone to a few stores before they found this one—a soft pink bed frame that was low to the ground. The mattress was covered with a waterproof cover, and had a matching pink sheet set and bedspread with little yellow flowers on it.

Beside the pillow was a fluffy decorative pillow shaped like a heart, and a stuffy that Matthew and Katie had picked out. Under the bed was a mesh bed guard they could easily put up if Abigail was worried about falling out of bed.

Across from Abigail's bed was Logan's crib. It was a Craftsman-inspired white solid wood crib and had an organic cotton mattress—Jaz had high-end taste in baby furniture. Jonathan chose a light blue crib blanket with soft patterns embroidered across it. "Once we find out what he loves, we'll get him another blanket," he decided after looking at blankets with everything from trucks to dinosaurs on them.

There was another stuffy from Matthew and Katie on Logan's bed. At Jenny's suggestion they had opted to not get a change table, figuring it was probably easier to just change Logan on the floor until he was toilet trained.

Max and Jenny had loaned them a white child's table with two chairs, a little white bookshelf, and a cheerful rainbow area rug and set up a little play area in the room. On the table was an unbreakable tea set, and the shelf held board books and toys. The walls were decorated with framed Winnie-the-Pooh prints, and a tall white dresser was filled with clothes for both kids. Lisa had anchored the dresser and the bookshelf to the wall once the room was set up.

Carrie turned on the little pink light that was clipped to Abigail's bed frame and turned off the main room light. Maisy flopped down beside her on the floor and put her head on her paws. Absentmindedly petting Maisy, Carrie finished her coffee and then meditated on the love she felt for the kids who would soon call this place home…

"Carrie. Morning."

The sound of Jonathan's voice drifted into Carrie's dreams. She opened her eyes and looked around before sitting up slowly. "Oh, hey!"

"It's a good thing you left a little light on in here or I would've had trouble finding you!" Jonathan sat beside her on Abigail's bed."

Carrie leaned on his shoulder. "What time is it?"

"Just six thirty. When did you come in here?"

"I think about an hour ago." She looked around the room. "Do we have the best friends or what?"

"I know. Everyone's done such an amazing job. And all kinds of things I wouldn't have considered! Like that grocery order Maria sent over yesterday with fun foods for the kids and all that baby stuff for Logan."

"I hadn't even thought of what he might eat," Carrie admitted. "He probably won't want to join you eating sushi for lunch for a while."

"It's OK. I can wait a few months for that."

"I have no idea how Matthew and Katie are going to make it through the school day. It was a good suggestion from Wendy to let the younger kids get a little used to you and I first, but if I was them I wouldn't be able to concentrate at all."

"So true. Care to follow me downstairs? I need coffee."

Carrie picked up her travel mug, straightened out the bed, and gave the room one last glance before turning off the lamp and following her husband downstairs. She turned on the outside light and let Maisy out for a pee. There were two new children's chairs in the glow of the light, along with a sit-on scooter shaped like a dump truck and some large, soft balls. All things her friends had brought over from their supply—or maybe even bought new. She wasn't sure. When Maisy bounded back, Carrie let her in and sat beside Jonathan at the island.

"You know what I was thinking last night?"

She shook her head.

"As soon as they're settled we need to do some family pictures. I love the ones we got done of us and the kids, but we need to update them so Abigail especially knows that she's part of the family."

Carrie looked up at one that was framed in their dining area. It was her favorite. Maisy was still a puppy, and the new-to-her environment the photographer had chosen for them was too much for her. No matter what they tried she wouldn't sit still. In the picture, they were all in different states of trying to get her to behave. It was a hilarious action shot where no one was looking at the photographer and it made her smile every time she looked at it.

"Well, at least now we know Maisy will stay still for photos. We should book the photographer for a month or two from now if we can. He's pretty popular."

Jonathan took out his phone and went on the photographer's website. In just a few minutes he had an outdoor session booked for two adults, four children, and a dog. "I still can't believe we're really doing this!"

CHAPTER 37

Carrie and Jonathan stood on the other side of the door, hands clasped together, as they waited for the doorbell to ring. When it did, Carrie slowly opened the front door. Wendy was standing there holding a squirming Logan and Abigail was standing beside her looking terrified. Dennis was a few feet behind them.

"Hello! Come on in!"

"Thanks!" Wendy reached out her hand to Abigail and they all walked into the house. "Abigail, Logan, this is Carrie and Jonathan. Remember when you played with them last week?"

Neither one answered, but Logan continued to squirm as Wendy crouched and set him down. Dennis closed the door behind them all and leaned against it looking completely relaxed.

Jonathan crouched in front of Logan. "Hey buddy. Can I help you take your jacket off?"

"I do it." Abigail said. She struggled a minute with the zipper before managing it and taking off the jacket.

Carrie pointed to the new hooks that had been added over the weekend. "There's a hook here for Logan's jacket, and one for yours right beside it."

Abigail hung up her brother's jacket. "Mine on." she announced.

Carrie shrugged. "OK. What about shoes?"

Abigail paused for a moment, before pushing Logan down onto his bottom and pulling off his shoes. As soon as they were off he was working to get himself standing up again. Abigail pulled off her own shoes and Carrie pointed to a mat under the jackets. "That's where we put ours."

Now standing, Logan made a few unbalanced steps towards the living room, saying 'Duh duh duh' as he went. Abigail was immediately by his side. Suddenly she let out an ear piercing scream and grabbed Logan. Maisy, who had been told to stay on her bed in the living room and was eagerly watching the new kids in her life, froze, her tail still.

Jonathan quickly placed himself between the kids and the dog. "That's Maisy. She's our dog. She's very, very gentle."

Abigail shook her head back and forth. "NO-NO-NO-NO-NO-NO-NO."

"It's OK. I'll put Maisy in our bedroom for now," Carrie said gently. She walked over to the dog. "Maisy, heel." Maisy immediately jumped up and stood at Carrie's side. Carrie took the furthest route possible around the two children before taking Maisy upstairs and shutting her in their room. Maisy looked confused. "Sorry girl," Carrie whispered.

When she came back downstairs Wendy apologized. "This is new to me—the dog thing."

Abigail seemed frozen, but Logan was working hard to get out of her tight grip and starting to whine. Carrie sat down on the floor beside Abigail, and Wendy sat on the other side. Jonathan and Dennis both sat on the couch. As soon as Logan escaped from his sister's arms he wobbled over to the coffee table and picked up a book.

"Do you like that one?" Jonathan asked. "Here, look." He touched the fuzzy surface on the cover and Logan followed his lead. "And look inside," Jonathan opened the book to the first page which was a different texture. Logan reached out to touch it and then looked at Jonathan as if to ask permission. "Go ahead, it's OK."

They had made their way through two more books before Abigail's curiosity overpowered her fear. She went and stood beside her brother and picked up the first book he had looked at. Slowly she touched each of the pages.

Carrie moved over to one of the shelves beside the fireplace and sat down on the floor again. She took out a few toys and laid them on the floor in front of her. Immediately Logan left the books and waddled over to her. He flopped down and picked up one of the stuffies. Abigail came over and grabbed it out of his hands before hugging it to her chest.

"Mine," she said to Logan. His lower lip trembled and Carrie quickly reached back for another one and gave it to him. He hugged it briefly before putting it down and reaching for a nubby ball.

"Most of the toys here are for everyone to play with," Carrie said softly. "There's a special stuffy just for you in your new room. Would you like to see?"

Abigail shook her head no and continued to hold the stuffie in one hand while reaching for a doll with the other hand. It had been one of Katie's favorites until recently, and Carrie had felt a little sad when it got relegated it to the basement storage area. At the time she had no idea another daughter would be holding it so soon.

"What do you think her name should be?" Carrie asked.

"I tink … I tink Sandra."

"Oh, OK. Well, what does Sandra think of this house?"

Abigail looked around. "Sandra want TV."

"Hmmm, can you tell Sandra that she can watch a bit of TV tomorrow morning? We don't watch much TV here. We like to play instead."

After pushing her hair away from her face, Abigail held the doll to her ear. "She want TV."

"How about a snack? What does Sandra like to eat?"

"Fishy crackers!"

Carrie breathed a sigh of relief. She must remember to thank Maria again for buying groceries. "Hey, we have fishy crackers. Do you want to take your jacket off now?" Abigail nodded, and walked with Carrie to the entrance to hang up her coat.

"OK, let's go get some fishy crackers." She waited to make sure Abigail would walk with her and slowly made her way to the kitchen where she pulled open the bottom drawer in the island. "Down here is plates, cups, and bowls just for you and Logan! Can you pick a bowl?"

She pulled out a purple one.

"Oh, what color did you choose?" Carrie asked.

"Pink!"

Curious, Carrie picked a blue bowl. "What color is this?"

This time Abigail paused. "Pink?"

"Let's get some fishy crackers in your bowl." Carrie unlocked the pantry and took out the package. "Look at all these yummy orange fishy crackers. And look! There's orange on the bag, too. Right here." She filled the bowl halfway. "Can you take that to the table?"

Abigail very slowly walked to the table and put the bowl down and the turned and looked at Carrie with a triumphant smile.

"Well done! Now, what would you like to drink?"

"Pink milk!"

Carrie assumed she meant strawberry milk. Well, that one she couldn't do. "I only have white milk sweetie. Is that ok or do you want apple juice?"

"Milk."

"OK. Do you think Logan would like some crackers and milk?"

"We're just coming to see." Jonathan said. He was walking with Logan who was hanging onto one of Jonathan's fingers with one hand and the wall with the other.

"Got it." Carrie got a small bowl of crackers for Logan and put milk in one of Katie's old sippy cups. Jonathan picked up Logan and put him in the highchair and then Carrie gave him his snack.

"He need bobble," Abigail said.

"Hmmm…" Jonathan said picking up the sippy cup. "Let's see what he thinks. Should I have a drink Logan?" He pretended to drink from the cup and Logan reached for it. "OK, you try it."

It took a few tries, and then Logan noisily started drinking.

"Carrie," Wendy said from the hallway where she was standing with Dennis and watching. "Are you OK to come with me to the car to bring in the kids' things?"

"Sure!"

"Dennis, can I make you a coffee or a tea or something?" Jonathan said, beginning to stand up.

"No thanks. You stay there with the kids."

Carrie grabbed her jacket and slipped on her boots, and Wendy did the same.

"Brrr," Carrie said when they stepped outside. "Not the best weather for kids to play outside. How do you think they'd do in one of the indoor play places?"

"It would probably overwhelm them both," Wendy admitted.

"They're not used to much stimulation." She opened her trunk and took out a garbage bag to hand to Carrie.

"Seriously? They sent the kids' stuff in garbage bags?"

"Yeah. It's the universal suitcase of the foster child I'm afraid." She grabbed another bag from the trunk and slammed it shut.

"That's it?"

"That's it. The rest of the things the kids were using belong to Henry and Sandra personally. Maybe we should take these things straight downstairs if that's where your washer is. Sandra did mention that with the short notice she had to put the dirty things in with the clean things."

"Thanks. I'll do that right away in case there's a toy or something they might want. How much do they know about their situation?"

"I told Abigail this morning that they were coming to live with the nice family they met last week and she could call you Mommy and Daddy if she wanted."

"Wow," Carrie said, opening the front door. "That seems pretty direct."

"I prefer to be as open as possible. But every case ends up being a little different."

"I'm just going to run these downstairs and start a load."

"Sure, I'll go check on things in the kitchen."

Downstairs Carrie tore open the bags and dumped them out on the floor. A quick sort revealed worn, but relatively clean clothes, two little blankets—one blue and one pink—and two stuffies. She got the blankets, stuffies, and most of the clothes into one load, and then walked up the stairs.

"One ... two ..."

"EEEEE!"

"Yes! Three!"

Carrie walked into the dining area to see Jonathan still beside Logan's highchair with all the fishy crackers in a line.

"Do you want to do it again?" he asked.

"Dah!" Logan nodded.

"OK." he pointed to the crackers, "One … two …"

"EEEEE!"

The adults chuckled. As soon as Abigail saw Carrie, she held up her bowl. "More!"

"More please," Carrie prompted. She could almost see Abigail battling with the suggestion.

"More … pease."

"Yes, for sure! Good manners! Do you think you can remember to say thank you when I give them to you?"

"Uh huh," she smiled.

This time Carrie filled the bowl full and placed it in front of Abigail, but kept a hand on it for a second.

"Tank you," Abigail said quietly.

"Yay! Good job! Do you give high fives?"

Abigail gave her a blank look.

"Like this," Jonathan said and held his hand up for Carrie to high five.

Abigail held hers up and Carrie tapped it. "High five is like a cheer!"

Logan held his up and Jonathan tapped it. Almost instantly both kids wanted to high five everyone in the room, and Carrie realized she had touched her new daughter for the first time.

A whining sound came from upstairs.

"Oh, that's Maisy, the dog," Carrie said casually. "I think she has to pee. Do you know where doggies go pee?"

Abigail shook her head no. Her eyes were already big and fearful.

Carrie lowered her voice to a stage whisper and leaned towards the little girl. "They pee outside. On the grass!" She was rewarded with a half-smile. "So I'm going to go upstairs and bring her down so she can go pee. And you can watch her out the window right from your chair! After Maisy goes pee, I'm going to put her on her bed. Do you see it in the corner there?"

Abigail leaned sideways to look, and nodded.

"Maisy is going to stay on that bed. She's not going to come over to you." She debated asking Abigail if it was OK for Maisy to stay downstairs, but decided it was a situation she should keep control of.

Maisy played the part of a well-trained dog perfectly. When she walked past the table Logan squealed and reached out to her, but she walked smartly right at Carrie's side until she was outside. When she came back in, Carrie gave her a minute to have a drink of water and then sent her to her doggy bed and told her to stay. Abigail watched the entire process with wide eyes.

Jonathan tried to get Logan to eat and drink in between counting crackers, but it was clear he wasn't interested in eating, only playing. In between, Wendy went over the legal forms they needed to sign, gave them identification cards for the kids, and explained what they could and could not do without permission from her. "It's also all written down. Please take time to read it through later tonight and if you have any questions, just call. If I'm not available ask for my supervisor."

"This is like a hand-off," Dennis explained. "From this point on, Wendy is your main social worker. But if anything comes up that you're not comfortable talking to her about, you're welcome to call me."

"Maybe the kids would like to see their bedroom," Wendy suggested.

Carrie looked at Abigail. "What do you think?"

"Doggy stay here?"

"Of course."

Jonathan showed Abigail how to open the gate at the bottom of the stairs, and then stood behind Logan to let him climb up on his own. But after two stairs he twisted around to sitting and reached his arms up. Jonathan picked him up right away, "Gonna have to work on the endurance buddy. You've got to keep up to everyone else!"

Carrie noticed that Abigail 'monkey climbed' the stairs and also seemed to struggle by the top two steps. They followed Jonathan and Logan through the gate at the top and paused for Wendy and Dennis.

"We'll always close this gate when we come up to keep Logan safe, OK?"

Abigail nodded.

"And this is your room here."

Jonathan put Logan down and he immediately waddled over to the shelf of toys and started pulling them down. Abigail went to her bed and gingerly reached out and touched the blanket, and then the soft pillow. She turned and looked at Carrie, looking uncertain.

"This is your bed sweetie," Carrie said with a smile.

Abigail looked down at the floor. "Pee pee," she whispered.

"Do you need to pee right now? The bathroom's right here."

She shook her head no and then pointed to the bed with tears in her eyes. "Pee pee," she whispered again.

Carrie kneeled down on the floor beside her. "Do you sometimes go pee pee in your bed?"

The little girl nodded, her chin quivering.

"That's OK. Look." Carrie lifted up the fitted sheet and showed her the waterproof pad underneath. "If you go pee pee in bed we can put everything in the laundry, and wipe this right here, and get you clean pajamas and clean blankets and it will be fine!" She made a mental note to text Jaz and ask for some extra sets of sheets and pajamas. "It's a pink bed, isn't it?"

"Pink bed. Abigail's."

"Yep. Abigail's pink bed."

Abigail turned to Carrie, put a hand on her shoulder, and looked her in the eye without blinking for what felt like an eternity. Then a squeal from Logan caught her attention and she went to explore the play area. Carrie felt like her entire world just stopped and shifted on its axis.

"I think Dennis and I are going to leave you now," Wendy said. "You're doing wonderful." She put her hand out to stop Jonathan from getting up. "It's OK. We'll let ourselves out." She crouched down beside Abigail. "I'm going to go now and you and Logan will stay here with your pink bed and your toys."

A few minutes later Carrie and Jonathan were vaguely aware of the sound of the front door closing. They were suddenly responsible for twice as many children.

CHAPTER 38

"What do you think about not having naps anymore?" Carrie asked Abigail at lunch. Jonathan had made hotdogs and raw fruit and vegetables for lunch with some cut bananas and soft cooked carrots for Logan. Abigail pushed the fruit and vegetables off her plate three times before Jonathan convinced her to leave them there and try a tiny bite of each.

Carrie and Jonathan were starting to use looks, winks, and hand gestures to decide what to try and encourage the kids to eat and what to let go. It was tricky to figure out what to push for, and they didn't want to start off with too many rules. While Logan loved being fed—for a few bites at least—he wasn't very good at feeding himself. Mealtimes were going to take a lot longer!

"No naps? Logan bees grumpy."

"*He* still needs a nap," Carrie agreed. "But maybe *you* don't."

"I no like naps ..." she took a bite of her hot dog and chewed for a bit. "No naps for Abigail?"

"No naps for Abigail."

"I be quiet. Stay in bed." She looked up, her eyes shining, "my pink bed!"

Jonathan stepped into the conversation, "You have a nice pink bed, but no naps means no bed. You can stay down here with us."

Carrie suddenly wondered if such a dramatic change from her schedule was too much. Maybe Sandra made her go for a nap because Abigail needed the down time. "What if you watch TV down here?"

"Logan nap now."

"In a little while." Carrie promised. "We'll play outside for a bit first."

"No wanna see ducks."

"OK. We'll go on the swings instead."

With the kids dressed for going outside, they went out in the back-yard. Jonathan grabbed a bag to clean up the dog poo, and then they let the kids explore. Logan had even more trouble walking with a coat on, so Carrie held his hand and tried to let him choose where to go.

Abigail went over to the swings and gave one a little push, and then cried out when it swung back and hit her in the arm. She backed up and gave the swings a wide berth. They watched her cautiously touch everything else and then come back to where Logan was trying to push a big ball.

"Logan nap now," she announced.

"We'll play a little more first," Carrie answered. She looked down at Logan. "Want to try the swing buddy?"

He looked up and said, "Duh."

She picked him up and carried him to the toddler swing that Max and Jenny had brought over and attached to the swing set. "Up we go!" Once he was secure in the swing she very carefully gave him a little push.

His eyes got wide. "Duh Duh DUH!" he said as he kicked his feet and tried to swing his body.

"Is that fun?" Carrie touched her fingers together in the sign for 'more'. "Do you want more?" she asked as she tapped her fingers together.

Logan clapped his hands.

"Good enough. More!" she said pushing the swing a little higher. He squealed, kicked his feet, and wiggled.

Carrie let the swing slow down. "Do you want more?" she asked, repeating the sign.

He looked at her for a second and then clapped his hands, and she proceeded to push him higher.

"OK, what are you doing?" Jonathan asked as he stood beside her.

Carrie explained about baby sign language and how it helped them communicate until they started talking.

"Wait a minute. We can teach him sign language?"

"Totally. It might be really good for him developmentally, especially if it gives him the power to communicate. I'll bet there's a class we can take together."

"That sounds like fun." He looked at Logan and touched his hands together a few times. "Do you want more?"

Logan nodded his head vigorously and clapped his hands.

"This is so cool!" he said as he pushed Logan.

Abigail came and stood beside the other swing. She looked up at Jonathan and did the sign for more.

"Are you asking for more too?" he asked.

She nodded.

"Good for you! You can help us teach your brother! But since you're a big girl, you can use your words, right?"

She nodded and repeated the sign.

"Sure you can go on the swing. Hop on and I'll give you a push."

Abigail gingerly held the swing with one hand and stood there.

"Here," Jonathan said, "can I help you get on?" She nodded and he gently lifted her into the swing. "Now hang on here and here. How's that?"

She wiggled her feet a little and smiled.

"Look at you! I'll give you a tiny push, and you say stop or more, OK?" He very gently pushed her, and then had to grab her when she almost fell backwards. "I got you. Keep hanging on with your hands, and try to keep your bottom on the seat, OK?"

Carrie pulled out her phone and took pictures of the two of them in between pushing Logan. She tried to get some of Logan too, but he was wiggling around so much with excitement that she wasn't sure if any of them would turn out. Wendy had assured them they could take all the pictures they wanted for themselves—just no sharing anywhere public.

Once Abigail got used to keeping her body in the swing she asked Jonathan to go higher and higher. He barely obliged, trying to be ready to catch her if she fell. And suddenly, for the first time, a giggle of pure joy came from her.

Carrie and Jonathan both heard it and agreed later that it was a turning point. Somewhere inside this serious, demanding, fearful child was a bright, happy little girl just waiting to come out.

They introduced the kids to the little slide and climbing wall before Logan started rubbing his eyes.

"I think it's time to get this guy upstairs for a nap," Carrie said. They went inside, took off all their outer clothes, had the kids wash their hands and drink some water, and got Abigail to use the bathroom. Then Carrie took Logan upstairs while Jonathan set up Abigail with a kids show.

Carrie came downstairs a few minutes later with a huge smile. "He was falling asleep before I could finish changing his diaper. I think that was more stimulation than he's used to."

"Want a coffee?" Jonathan asked.

"Please." She went to let Maisy out, who had obediently stayed on her bed. It didn't feel fair to the dog who lived to be with 'her' kids. When Maisy came in, Carrie picked up her bed and moved it into the living room where it was as far away as possible from Abigail while still in her sight line. "Maisy's going to stay right here to keep you safe," she said to Abigail.

Aside from lifting her feet onto the couch and scooting into the corner, Abigail didn't give any indication she heard.

Carrie went to join Jonathan at the island where they could see into the living room and keep an eye on things.

"Would it be too much for us to take them to the big playground when the older kids are home from school?" he asked quietly.

"No, I think we need to gently push them so they can build up some endurance. We can have snack first and then all head out."

"What about Maisy?"

"She needs to come too, but maybe you or I could walk ahead with her. It might help Abigail to see all the kids coming up and petting her. And at the playground we can all take turns walking around with Maisy. It will give Maisy a little attention and give Abigail exposure that isn't threatening." Carrie wondered if Abigail would ever be able to tell her why she was afraid of dogs. Did something happen? Or had she always been like that?

"Sounds like a good idea."

With Abigail occupied and Logan fast asleep Carrie and Jonathan each got out their laptops to try and get a little work done. After an hour had passed and another show ended, Carrie went over and turned off the TV.

"That's enough TV. Do you want to do a puzzle? Or play a game?"

Abigail stood on the couch. "TV ON!"

"Not right now. Here, come see what you want to play with —"

Abigail slipped from the couch, landed on the floor, and started screaming. Carrie and Jonathan were there instantly.

"Is she hurt?" he asked, kneeling beside her.

"I don't think so," Carrie had to raise her voice to be heard. "She landed on her feet and then dropped to the floor." She tried to put her hand on Abigail's forehead. "Hey sweetie, you're OK."

Abigail stopped for a moment, looked Carrie in the eye, and then flopped flat on the floor, opened her mouth wide and continued screaming while she banged her hands and feet.

"Oh," Carrie said. "I see." She motioned to Jonathan and moved to the hallway where she could see Abigail out of the corner of her eye without looking at her.

"What are you doing? What if she's hurt?" Jonathan asked.

"If she was hurt she probably wouldn't be able to stop and take a breath. I think this is the way she tantrums. Wendy mentioned something like this." Carrie smacked her hand on her forehead. "Shoot! This is my fault. I didn't give her any warning before turning off the TV!"

Jonathan ran his hands through his hair. "But we still don't want her to have tantrums. And she's going to wake up Logan!"

"I'm trying to think of how to handle this… Let's just ignore it and when she calms down we can go to her."

A little voice upstairs started calling, "Duh Duh Duh."

"Well, this tantrum thing is freaking me out," Jonathan admitted. "I'll go get Logan and play with him upstairs until it's safe to come down. Do I need to change his diaper?"

"Only if it feels loaded," Carrie said. "I'll be at the island I guess. I can't see her on the floor, but I'll see if she gets up."

"Good luck!"

A few minutes later Carrie carefully walked into the quiet living room. Abigail was still lying on the floor. Her face was red and her hair was everywhere. Carrie sat down beside her on the floor and gently moved her hair off her forehead.

"Hey there," she said quietly. "Were you upset that I turned off the TV?"

Abigail nodded.

"I'm sorry. Sometimes the TV will get turned off, but next time I'll remember to give you a warning first so you have some time to be ready. OK?"

Another nod.

"But in this house, when we don't like something we use our words, not screaming and kicking. So if there's something you don't like, you come tell us what you don't like. We will always listen to your words." She continued to gently stroke Abigail's hair and the little girl's eyes started to close.

"Abigail, would you like a little snuggle?"

She opened her eyes and looked at Carrie for almost a full minute before slowly nodding.

"OK, but I'm too old to be on the floor for a long time. Come here." She stood up and carefully helped Abigail up and then sat on the couch and placed her daughter on her lap. Abigail sat stiffly, so Carrie started stroking her hair again. When Abigail's eyes started to close, Carrie very slowly put her arms around her and hugged her. The little body sagged into hers and Carrie felt her eyes filling with tears. She couldn't have described the emotion she was feeling.

When Jonathan came down carrying Logan, Abigail was sound asleep in Carrie's arms. His eyes widened, and then filled with tears, too. Pulling his phone out, he took a picture. "I'm going to see if I can figure out if he wants to eat or drink anything," he whispered.

Carrie nodded. She rested her head on the couch and closed her eyes. The sound of Jonathan asking Logan questions and Logan answering everything with a 'Duh' made her smile.

CHAPTER 39

"Abigail. Abigail sweetie, it's time to wake up." Carrie didn't want to end the moment with Abigail, but the kids would be home in fifteen minutes and she didn't want her to be startled when they came in the door. Ken had offered to pick them both up and drop them off after school today.

Slowly Abigail's eyes opened and she looked around in confusion.

"You're at your new house now with Logan. And you had a little snuggle! It was nice." Abigail rested her head back on Carrie's shoulder, so she waited a few minutes before trying again. "OK sweetie. Time to wake up." She sat up a little and Abigail sat up and rubbed her eyes. "Do you need to go potty?" Carrie got a grunt in response that probably meant 'no'. "Let's just walk over there then. You don't have to go."

She held Abigail's hand as they walked into the main floor bathroom. Once they were there Abigail pulled down her pants and climbed on the toilet to pee. Carrie tried not to get upset at how worn her underwear was. There was an entire set of brand new underwear upstairs that Abigail could choose from in the morning.

After washing their hands they went back into the kitchen where Logan was happily playing in the large plastics drawer while Jonathan cut up fruit for snack. Abigail immediately joined Logan on the floor, and Carrie went over and kissed Jonathan's cheek.

"Nice parenting so far," he said quietly.

"Right back atcha' there!" She went and sat on the floor with the kids. "In a few minutes Matthew and Katie will be home. They're the kids you played with last week. They're very excited to see you again."

No response.

"When they come home from school we always have a snack. Does that sound like a good idea?"

"Duh!" Logan said.

"I agree buddy!" Carrie said, pushing his hair to the side. He was definitely in need of a haircut. So was Abigail for that matter. Wendy had told them they could take the kids to the hairdresser—something Carrie hadn't realized they might need permission for. And in the instructions Wendy had left with them was a note to get both kids in for a checkup with the doctor, and the dentist and eye doctor for Abigail. Fortunately, Sandra had provided their vaccination records, which were up to date.

The front door opened. "Hello?" Katie called in an unusually quiet voice.

Jonathan quickly went to the front door and Carrie reached a hand to each of the kids. "Let's go say hi!" They made their way to the entrance, where Matthew and Katie were taking off their shoes and coats.

"Maisy!" Matthew said, and Maisy immediately jumped up and trotted over, delighted to be out of her imposed sitting session. Abigail immediately tried to go behind Carrie to hide and Carrie had to let go of Logan so she didn't lose her balance. She turned around and picked Abigail up and Logan plopped on his bottom.

Maisy took her chance to sniff him, her tail wagging furiously. Logan giggled and reached for her ears.

"NO, NO!" Abigail yelled.

Carrie took a few steps back with her. "It's OK. Maisy is gentle. Logan likes her, see? And look, Katie and Matthew can pet her and she likes it." The kids both went to Maisy.

Katie kneeled down beside Logan. "Do you like our doggy?" she asked as she wrapped her arms around Maisy's neck.

Matthew scratched Maisy's ears and looked at Abigail. "She's very soft. Do you want to pet her?"

Abigail shook her head vigorously.

"Why don't you two wash up and then we'll have snack," Carrie said. "We'll wash our hands in the kitchen, OK?" Abigail wrapped her arms tightly around Carrie's neck. After a bit of a struggle her hands got washed.

Matthew and Katie came into the dining area each holding one of Logan's hands.

"Look Mommy!" Katie said. "Logan's a good walker!"

"He is," Carrie agreed, still holding Abigail. "Here, I'm going to put your at your special pink chair, and Maisy's going to have a little treat that she can eat on her bed." She pried Abigail's hands away and sat her on the booster seat. "Katie and Matthew will sit on either side of you, OK?"

She put Maisy's bed back in the dining area and gave her a dental bone to chew while Jonathan put little plates out at each spot and a tray of fruit. He already had a bowl of soft fruits for Logan ready near his highchair. "Up we go buddy!"

"Duh!"

"What does that mean?" Matthew asked.

"So far, it means everything!" Jonathan said smiling. "Your mom said we can teach him sign language and then he can start communicating with us that way."

"Cool!"

"Exactly what I said," Jonathan answered, reaching up for a high five. Logan put his hand in the air too and Jonathan gave him a high five. "I think high fives are his first party trick."

Katie slid the tray closer. "What do you want?" she asked Abigail.

"Fishy crackers!"

"We had those for a snack earlier, didn't we?" Carrie said. "Katie, what's your favorite fruit?"

"Strawberries! Want one?" she asked Abigail.

She nodded and Katie put two on her plate before grabbing a handful for herself. "I like bananas, and oranges, and blueberries too! Well, I didn't used to like blueberries but I do now! Do you want one?"

Again, Abigail nodded.

"Here, eat one!" Katie said, popping one into her own mouth. "Yummy!"

Abigail put it in her mouth and bit down before opening her mouth and letting the berry and the juice run back out.

"Oops!" Carrie said, reaching for a napkin. She came behind Abigail and wiped her mouth and shirt. "Guess you weren't used to that. It's OK."

"When you're eight you'll like blueberries," Katie assured her. "Mommy, can I tell about my day first?"

"Matthew, is that OK with you?"

"Mmmmhmmm," he said with a mouthful of banana.

"Go ahead Katie."

In between bites she gave a rundown of everything that had happened at school. Abigail seemed to be hanging on every word, and Carrie took the chance to slip one of each fruit onto her plate.

"And tomorrow is Jane's birthday and she said she's bringing cupcakes for everyone!" Katie finished.

"I go school?" Abigail asked.

Jonathan had been putting fruit on a plastic spoon and helping Logan eat. He looked at Carrie.

"Soon," Carrie promised. Figuring out when to start her in preschool might be tricky, but she definitely needed some school experience before starting kindergarten in the fall.

Matthew and Katie continued to help themselves to food as Matthew talked a little about his day. "I have the band trip permission form in my bag. Are we OK to pay the deposit?"

"Of course! Does it need signing too?"

"Yep. I'll get it in a sec," he said as he reached for a handful of cut apples. "I'm still hungry. Can I have some peanut butter with these?"

"No peanut butter for now. We don't know what Logan might be allergic too. What about some cheese?"

"Yeah, sure."

Carrie got up to cut some cheese into cubes. "Abigail? Do you want a piece of cheese?"

"Ya!"

"Yes please?" Carrie prompted.

"Yes pease."

"Good job! Eat one bite from your plate and I'll bring you some cheese."

She looked at her plate warily before picking up a slice of banana and eating it. Carrie thought she was going to gag for a moment.

"Yay!" Katie cheered. "Good job Abby!"

Abigail smiled. "Abby."

"Yeah, you can be Abby! Abby and Katie! Abby and Katie!" Katie said in a sing song voice.

"Abby and Katie!" Abigail repeated.

"EEEEE!" Logan shouted.

Katie giggled. "What does that mean?"

"I think he wants to play the counting game! I played it with him this morning. Let's see," Jonathan lined up three pieces of fruit on the highchair tray. "One … two …"

"EEEEE!"

"Yes, three!" he said, and put the third piece on the spoon and guided it to Logan's mouth.

"Mommy! Logan can count! He can count!" Katie bounced in her chair. "I'm going to tell everyone tomorrow that my little brother can count!"

"I count too," Abigail said.

Katie turned to her. "Do you want to count fruit, like your brother?" Without waiting for an answer she lined up all the fruit on Abigail's tray. "OK, what's this one?" She pointed to the first fruit.

"One …" Katie moved to the next one.

"Two …" Katie moved to the third one.

"Eeeee" This time, Katie looked at Jonathan. He nodded his chin to the next one and Katie pointed to it.

"One!"

"Um … good job Abby!"

Carrie came over with a plate of cheese cubes. She put three on Abigail's plate, three on Logan's tray, and then put the plate between Matthew and Katie. They both took a handful.

"Thanks Mom!" Matthew said.

Abigail shoved all three in her mouth and reached for more.

"Hang on sweetie. Finish what's in your mouth first and then you can ask for more."

She swallowed quickly. "More."

Katie leaned over. "Remember to say please," she whispered.

"Pease," Abigail whispered. They all laughed.

"Good job! Go ahead and take some."

She grabbed the last two and shoved them in her mouth.

"What are we going to do after snack Mommy?" Katie asked.

"We thought we'd go to the big playground. Abigail and Logan had lots of fun in the back yard this morning."

"Ooohhh, I love the big playground," Katie told Abigail. "It's got swings, and monkey bars, and a spinny thing, and a slide! And if my friends are there you can meet them!"

Abigail nodded.

At the playground, Jonathan and Carrie ended up standing back from the kids with Maisy. Katie was pushing Logan on the baby swing and making faces every time he swung towards her, making him laugh.

Matthew was helping Abigail get up the climbing wall, patiently showing her where to put her hands, and encouraging her loudly every time she moved up a little bit.

Jonathan reached down to pat Maisy. "Well, this feels …"

"Like a movie?" Carrie suggested.

"Weirder than a movie. Yesterday we had two kids. Today we have four."

"I wonder how long it will take to feel like our normal."

He smiled, "I thought you said, 'normal was boring' to Katie the other day."

"It is. And I could almost do with some boring already. The kids are fantastic, but they're so far behind. Especially Abby. Abigail. I don't know what to call her!" she laughed.

"I like Abby. It feels like it suits her more than Abigail."

"It kind of does. I mean, based on the seven hours we've known her so far."

Jonathan pulled out his phone and took a few candid pictures of the kids playing. "Do you think we could send these to our family and friends?"

"Yeah. Wendy just said nothing public. Maybe remind everyone again that they can't share them or anything."

He nodded. "Good point."

"Daddy! I think Logan's done!"

"Coming!" he said, handing Maisy's leash to Carrie.

That night, Carrie and Jonathan sat on their loveseat with a glass of sparkling wine each.

"I'm not sure we should be celebrating after just one day," he admitted.

"Are you kidding? We have four kids who stayed alive all day and who are all tucked in their beds sleeping now. Of course we should. Today was scary."

"Terrifying," he added.

"And pretty darn amazing," she said with a smile.

"Yeah. But I was wondering … how on earth will you manage when I have to travel next month?"

She looked at him, eyes narrowing. "You're kidding, right?"

"Uh, yes? No? What's the answer?"

She laughed. "I'll be fine. Yes, there will be growing pains, but I'm not the first mom to spend a day alone with four kids. Not to mention Matthew and Katie will be a huge help."

He sighed. "You're right. But I feel bad when I think about leaving."

She leaned against him. "You should. You should feel very, very bad."

"I'll make it up to you in *whatever* way you want."

"Good to know. I'll make a list."

"I love you Carrie Brandt, amazing mother of four kids."

"And I love you too Jonathan Brandt, amazing father of four kids!"

A NOTE FROM THE AUTHOR

Phew! Writing this book took me on quite an emotional journey! While the situations are a combination of numerous adoption stories and experiences and are not based on my specific journey, they brought up many memories of my own experiences as an adoptive mom.

If you are living through infertility, considering adoption, or longing for children to fill your home, I'm sending extra love and good thoughts to you! Please, reach out to others in this time. You do not need to walk this journey alone.

There are also some amazing foster parents out there, loving the kids that come and go through their homes. You are fantastic! Thank you!

And to all the adoptees out there: you make our lives full by walking the incredibly scary and brave journey of joining a new home and a new family. Thank you for being, for trying, for loving, for growing, for forgiving, and for being you.

Finally, thank you to the children of my heart: Alyssa, Jayce, Avery, and Tianna. Because of you, I get the most incredible name on earth—Mom.

* * *

I'm so excited to offer a free, exclusive epilogue for my readers! It's not available for sale—the only way to receive it is to sign up here:

https://BookHip.com/VVFMAA

In a few short minutes you can be reading more! Enjoy your free download. (You'll automatically be on my newsletter list too, but you're welcome to unsubscribe at any time.)

Thank you for reading *Growing By Four Feet*! If you have two free minutes, would you please leave a review? Reviews are an author's best friend and like rocket fuel for a book!

For regular posts and updates, follow me on Facebook:

fb.me/CarmenKlassen.Author

May all your days be full of good books, nice people, and happy endings.

Sincerely,

Carmen

fb.me/CarmenKlassen.Author